CAN NIGHTMARES COME TRUE?

Melanie was surrounded by girls. Katie. Beth. Christie. And Jana. And they were all frowning at her and shaking their heads.

"We don't like you anymore," said Katie. "You never talk about anything *we* want to talk about."

"We don't want to be friends anymore," said Beth. "We've all made new friends."

"*Better* friends," said Christie.

"The Fabulous Five is through!" said Jana.

Melanie tried to talk to them, but no words would come out. She tried to shout, but she couldn't make a sound. Finally, she reached out toward them and POOF! All four of them vanished into thin air.

Just then a high-pitched sound echoed in her mind. She opened her eyes and recognized the bell ringing to end the class. All around her, kids were scrambling for the door, but Melanie sat still for a while, unable to shake off the effects of the dream.

"What if it wasn't a dream?" she whispered, and then shuddered. "What if it was a premonition?"

THE FABULOUS FIVE

The Kissing Disaster

BETSY HAYNES

A BANTAM SKYLARK BOOK®
TORONTO • NEW YORK • LONDON • SYDNEY • AUCKLAND

RL 5, 009–012

THE KISSING DISASTER
A Bantam Skylark Book / April 1989

Skylark Books is a registered trademark of Bantam Books, a division of Bantam Doubleday Dell Publishing Group, Inc. Registered in U.S. Patent and Trademark Office and elsewhere.

ISBN 0-553-15710-8

Published simultaneously in the United States and Canada

Bantam Books are published by Bantam Books, a division of Bantam Doubleday Dell Publishing Group, Inc. Its trademark, consisting of the words "Bantam Books" and the portrayal of a rooster, is Registered in U.S. Patent and Trademark Office and in other countries. Marca Registrada. Bantam Books, 666 Fifth Avenue, New York, New York 10103.

PRINTED IN THE UNITED STATES OF AMERICA

CW   0 9 8 7 6 5 4 3 2 1

The
Kissing
Disaster

CHAPTER

1

Melanie Edwards stifled a yawn. Biology class sure was boring. She tuned out the lecture and started to study her teacher instead. Mr. Dracovitch was tall and thin with a pale complexion, and he wore a toupee that was too dark and too shiny and was always pulled down too far on his forehead. It was no wonder that the kids called him Dracula behind his back, she mused, and made up gruesome stories about what happened to the poor creatures in the cages lining the walls of his biology lab. There were a variety of rodents such as mice and hamsters, plus two crows and a green garden snake.

1

"Class, tomorrow you will begin dissecting the eyeball of a cow."

Mr. Dracovitch's announcement pierced Melanie's dreamlike trance and made her sit up abruptly. The eyeball of a *cow!* she wanted to shriek.

In the seat beside her, Elizabeth Harvey made a face and moaned, "E-e-e-*y-e-w*."

"Gross!" and "Yuck!" came from several directions, and Shawnie Pendergast turned green, covered her mouth with both hands, and made a quick dash out of the room.

Mr. Dracovitch waited for the furor to die down before speaking again. "Yes, you heard me right. I did say the eyeball of a cow. But I guarantee that you'll all be fascinated by what we learn, and I want you to read Chapter Thirteen in your textbooks tonight in preparation."

Melanie looked longingly at the door through which Shawnie had made her exit. Her own stomach had lurched a couple of times, too. *Cut up the eyeball of a cow?* Maybe her mild-mannered biology teacher *was* the infamous Count Dracula, after all.

"For this project," Mr. Dracovitch went on, "I will divide the class into teams. Each team will consist of two students and will have one eyeball to dissect together."

Melanie was certain she saw an eyebrow raise menacingly when he said the word "eyeball," and she shuddered at the thought of actually having to touch such a thing.

"These students will be partners," Mr. Dracovitch said. "Bill Soliday and Sara Sawyer. Eric Silverman and Elizabeth Harvey. Tammy Lucero and Chandra Sharp. Shawnie Pendergast and Joel Murphy. Shane Arrington and Melanie Edwards. . . ."

Melanie shot to attention for the second time. Shane Arrington was going to be her partner? Cool, gorgeous Shane? He was one of several boys she had crushes on, and he was definitely the most interesting. His parents were hippies, which probably accounted for his laid-back personality, and he had a pet iguana named Igor, whom he claimed was his best friend. On top of that, he could pass for River Phoenix's identical twin any day of the week. It would be worth touching the eye-ball of a cow to be partners with Shane. Well, she thought, almost.

Catching her glance from across the room, Shane gave her a thumbs-up signal. Melanie returned it with a smile and then looked quickly at Tammy Lucero to see if she had noticed. She had, Melanie thought gleefully. Tiny, dark-haired Tammy had the reputation of being the biggest gossip in the seventh grade. Usually that was a pain, but not now. Tammy was also a member of The Fantastic Foursome, the clique that was the rival of The Fabulous Five, which was what Melanie and her four best friends had called them-selves since fifth grade. Laura McCall, the leader of The Fantastic Foursome, had a big crush on Shane. Naturally Tammy would report back to Laura that Melanie and Shane were partners.

Melanie could hardly wait to meet her friends at Bumpers after school and tell them about the project and about Shane. It seemed strange to be the only member of The Fabulous Five to be taking biology. In Mark Twain Elementary they had done absolutely everything together, even though they had totally different personalities.

She knew that her friends thought she was boy crazy because she had crushes on so many boys. She could almost hear Katie telling her so for the zillionth time when she heard how excited Melanie was to have Shane for her biology partner. Melanie put up with their opinions in silence, even though she considered herself romantic—not boy crazy.

Certainly she was more romantic than Katie Shannon, who was a feminist and a member of Wakeman Junior High's newly organized Teen Court. Katie pretended not to like boys at all, but everybody knew that she secretly liked Tony Calcaterra.

Jana Morgan, the unofficial leader of The Fabulous Five, was a little bit romantic. Her boyfriend was Randy Kirwan, who was one of the nicest, handsomest, and most popular boys in seventh grade. Jana even admitted once that she used to keep a poster-size picture of Randy on her bedroom wall so that she could gaze at it while she fell asleep at night.

Beth Barry was too busy acting theatrical to be romantic. She and Keith Masterson went out sometimes, but mostly she talked about Drama Club and about the plight of the American Indians.

Melanie used to think that Christie Winchell, the fifth member of the clique, was romantic, but that was when she and Jon Smith had first started seeing a lot of each other. Now it seemed that all they did was play tennis. How romantic could that be?

Her friends' attitudes toward boys and romance were more than Melanie could understand, but they were still her best friends, and she rushed into Bumpers after school, anxious to find them and tell them her news. In the doorway she hesitated for a moment. Things hadn't been quite the same between them lately. Katie was preoccupied with Teen Court, and Jana spent half her time with Funny Hawthorne, her seventh-grade coeditor on the yearbook. But wait until I tell them about the cow's eye, she thought. They'll absolutely die.

Bumpers was noisy, as usual. The after-school crowd from Wacko, as most kids called Wakeman Junior High, filled the booths, tables, and bumper cars to overflowing, and kids gathered in the aisles, beside the order counter, and around the huge old Wurlitzer jukebox. The brightly painted bumper cars were relics from an ancient amusement park ride and had given the fast-food restaurant its name.

"Hi, Mel," someone called as she pushed her way through the crowd.

"Hi, Alexis," she called back to Alexis Duvall, who was sitting at a crowded table and was almost hidden by the tidal wave of kids surging past.

"Listen, Melanie," Alexis shouted. "Are you going

to the meeting about the seventh-grade dance in the morning?"

Melanie nodded. There was going to be a dance just for seventh-graders in a month, and the first meeting for kids interested in helping organize it and serving on committees was being held before school the next morning. As excited as Melanie was about the dance, she was more interested in talking to her friends right now.

"Can't talk now," she said apologetically. "Have you seen any of The Fabulous Five?"

"Over there," said Alexis, raising one arm like a periscope and pointing toward the far corner of the room.

Melanie nodded and lip-synched "thank you" along with the lyrics of a song blasting from the jukebox. Alexis was breaking up with laughter as Melanie headed toward her friends.

"Hi, gang. Guess what?" she yelled above the noise as she slid into the booth beside Jana.

"Hi, Melanie," said Jana. "Gosh, would you let me out? I need to talk to Funny about some yearbook stuff."

"Don't you want to hear my big news?" asked Melanie.

"I'd love to, Mel, but can't it wait? I really have to talk to Funny. It's important."

Without answering, Melanie slid out of the booth.

"Thanks," said Jana. "See you later."

Melanie frowned at the back of Jana's head and then sat down again, scooting toward Christie.

"You won't believe what old Dracula told us today," Melanie said to Christie, who was staring at a spot on the table. "We're going to have to dissect the eyeball of a cow. Isn't that gross?" She waited for Christie's reaction.

Christie didn't look up. It's awfully noisy, Melanie thought. Maybe she simply hadn't heard. Then Melanie noticed a faraway look in her eyes.

"Christie," said Melanie, bending closer to her friend. "Earth to Christie. Do you read me?"

"Oh, hi, Melanie." Christie's eyes came into focus and she looked surprised to see Melanie sitting there. "Maybe you can give me some advice."

Melanie shrugged. "Sure. If I can."

"It's about Jon," Christie began. "I can't decide if I should help him out on his tennis serve or pretend I don't know what he's doing wrong and keep on beating him. I know winning isn't everything, but it's sure fun. What do you think?"

"Isn't that sort of cheating?" snapped Melanie. Christie hadn't heard a single word she had said about Mr. Dracovitch and the biology project. She had been too busy thinking about Jon and his tennis serve.

"Mmmmm." Christie nodded and drifted back into her dreamy state.

Melanie was fuming. She hated being ignored, especially by her best friends. Well, maybe Katie and Beth would listen, she thought. But when she glanced across the table to where they had been sitting only moments before, they were gone. They had vanished into thin air. Two of her best friends in the whole world had left without so much as a word.

Melanie slumped against the back of the booth. Nobody seemed to care about *her* anymore. Not one of her friends wanted to hear what she had to say. The same thing had already happened twice this week and a couple of times last week. Those other times she had thought that maybe what she had to talk about was just too boring. *But dissecting the eyeball of a cow?* How could anybody call that boring?

Melanie scooted out of the booth and headed for the door. She thought about stopping to talk to Alexis about the dance but changed her mind. Even though Alexis seemed interested in talking to her—unlike *some* people she could name—she wanted to get out of there. She had to think about the awful question that had been nagging at her lately. Was it possible that after all The Fabulous Five had meant to each other, they were starting to break up?

CHAPTE

2

*A*fter dinner Melanie turned to Chapter 13 in her biology book, but she couldn't concentrate on the assignment. Her thoughts kept turning to stories she had heard about how different things were in junior high and how sometimes friendships changed or, even worse, ended altogether.

In elementary school everyone had known everybody else, and friendships had been special. But suddenly in junior high, things weren't the same anymore. Seventh-graders came together from several schools around town, and sometimes you wouldn't have a single class with your best friends, or for that matter, with

9

...e you knew. It could be pretty lonely at
...l you made some new friends. Maybe that
...what was happening to the other members of The
...abulous Five. They were making new friends and
leaving her behind.

Take Jana, for instance, she thought. Until lately
Jana had always been the problem solver, the one who
could keep the group together. But now she was spending most of her time working on the yearbook, *The
Wigwam*, with her new friend Funny Hawthorne. She
hardly had any time for The Fabulous Five anymore.

The same went for Christie. She used to prefer her
Fabulous Five friends over the tennis court, where her
father was trying to turn her into a professional player.
Now she was spending every waking moment playing
tennis with Jon Smith.

Katie couldn't talk about anything except the cases
that came before Teen Court and how she was wiping
out problem behavior at Wakeman Junior High practically single-handedly. What she wouldn't talk about
was Tony Calcaterra, the repeat offender who had a
crush on her.

Even Beth had gone off on a tangent lately. Ever
since she had met Trevor Morgan, the lead singer with
the rock group Brain Damage, and found out how
badly American Indians had been treated, she was trying to help educate the public about it. Beth hadn't
given the American Indians a second thought back in
Mark Twain Elementary. She had mostly only cared
about her friends.

The Fabulous Five had been a real club then with weekly meetings on Saturday afternoons in Jana's bedroom. They had collected dues and had T-shirts printed that said THE FABULOUS FIVE across the front, and they had worn them to the meetings. Everybody in school had known how special their friendship was. But now, they went to football games on Saturday afternoons, and there didn't seem to be time for meetings. They had outgrown their old T-shirts and had not gotten around to getting new ones. And Melanie couldn't help wondering if their friendship was special anymore.

She yawned and noticed that while she had been thinking about her friends she was also doodling in the margins of the page in her biology book showing a diagram of a cow's eye. She winced. She should be reading Chapter 13. Dracula would expect everyone in the class to know what was going on tomorrow. He might even pop a quiz.

"So what?" she said out loud, slapping the book shut. "Saving The Fabulous Five is more important than any old cow's eye, quiz or no quiz. This is a crisis."

Melanie bounded down the stairs and headed for the kitchen phone. She knew she should get permission from her parents for what she was about to do, but they had taken her six-year-old brother, Jeffy, out for ice cream. It was a reward for not crying when the pediatrician had given him a booster shot earlier in the day. First things first, she thought as she dialed Jana's number and listened to it ring. She would talk to her mom and dad later.

She hardly gave Jana time to say hello. "Jana, this is Melanie. I'm having a sleepover Saturday night. I thought we'd have a Fabulous Five meeting at the stroke of midnight. Stuff like that. Can you come?"

"Wow, Melanie, that sounds great. The only trouble is . . ." Jana's voice trailed off, and Melanie braced herself for what was coming. "I promised Mom and Pink that I'd go bowling with them. They go every Saturday night. Remember?"

"Oh, sure," mumbled Melanie. *Remember*—how could she forget? Jana was always complaining about how boring it was that her mother and new stepfather never did anything else on Saturday night. They went bowling week after week after week. And now she was going along? It was incredible.

"Anyway, Pink is going to teach me how to throw something besides gutter balls," Jana added with a nervous laugh. "I think it's going to be fun."

After they hung up, Melanie reminded herself that ever since her mother's marriage to Pink, Jana had seemed preoccupied with adjusting to the new situation at home. Maybe that was why she was going bowling with them, Melanie reasoned, *not* because she had lost interest in The Fabulous Five.

Next Melanie called Katie. "How about sleeping over at my house Saturday night?" she asked, trying to sound cheerful.

"I'd love to, but Teen Court is having a pizza party

Saturday night," said Katie. "I thought I told every-body."

"You didn't tell me," Melanie grumbled. But then, nobody tells me *anything* anymore, she thought of adding. Instead she asked, "Is Tony Calcaterra going to be there?"

"Of course not," Katie insisted. "This party is just for judges."

"Oh, right," said Melanie slyly. "He just gets into trouble and has to come before the court so often that I've started thinking of him as a member. Talk to you later. Bye."

Melanie hung up before Katie could blow her stack. Everybody teased Katie about Tony. She had a crush on him, too. She just wouldn't admit it.

She punched in Christie's phone number a little slower than she had the other two. Christie was proba-bly going out with Jon on Saturday night. Still, she reasoned, it wouldn't hurt to ask.

"Oh, rats," said Christie upon hearing Melanie's in-vitation. "Wouldn't you know it? That just happens to be the night when Jon's parents invited us to the TV station to sit in on an interview they're taping to play on the air Sunday afternoon."

Melanie sighed with irritation. Jon's parents were Chip Smith and Marge Whitworth, both big-deal per-sonalities on the local television station.

"Boris Becker is coming through town," Christie went on excitedly, "and it's the chance of a lifetime to meet him. You do know who Boris Becker is, don't you?"

"Of course," huffed Melanie. Everybody knew who Boris Becker was. He was the German tennis star who had taken Wimbledon and a bunch of other big tournaments while he was still a teenager. Everyone had heard of him.

There was only one person left to call: Beth. Melanie grabbed a handful of brownies from the plate on the counter and stared at the phone. Should she risk rejection again? she asked herself as she stuffed an entire brownie into her mouth. Four times in one evening was a lot of rejection to handle. Still, she had to do something to keep The Fabulous Five together.

Beth's father answered and went to call Beth to the phone. While she waited, Melanie listened to the racket in the background. Music was playing. People were talking. Agatha was barking. What a madhouse, she thought. But then with five kids and an Old English sheepdog in the family, it wasn't surprising.

"Hi, Mel. Sorry to keep you waiting."

Beth's chirpy voice lifted Melanie's spirits slightly, and she said, "Would you like to sleep over at my house Saturday night? I don't know what we'll do. Everybody else is busy, and it will probably be boring."

"Great. What time?"

Melanie frowned at the phone. Had she heard wrong? "What did you say?" she asked incredulously.

"I said, great. What time?"

"How does six-thirty sound?" Her heart was pounding. Beth was actually saying yes.

"It sounds terrific. I'll be there."

Melanie danced around the room after she hung up. Maybe it wasn't too late for The Fabulous Five after all. She would make Saturday night so much fun that Beth would talk the ears right off their other three friends.

"What should we eat?" she whispered as she got paper and pencil and plopped onto the stool at the end of the kitchen counter. "Pizza? No, that's too common. Hamburgers? Too much trouble to fix. Lobs-tah Newburg and cavi-ah, dhaling?" she drawled, and began to giggle.

Just then the phone rang. Stifling her laughter, Melanie picked up the receiver. "Hello."

"Hi, Mel. It's Beth again. About Saturday night . . ."

Melanie's heart dropped into her shoes. "What about it?" she asked softly.

"Gosh. I feel awful," Beth began, "but I just looked at Mom's calendar, and I'm supposed to stuff envelopes that night."

"*Stuff envelopes?*" Melanie shrieked.

"Yeah, at the Indian mission. They're writing letters to Congress about some land they say was stolen from some tribes over a hundred years ago. I promised I'd help. You understand, don't you?"

"Of course," Melanie sniffed.

She hung up and stared at the kitchen floor for a

long time as she slowly finished the brownies. Jana was going bowling. Katie was having pizza with the Teen Court. Christie was going to a television taping. And Beth was stuffing envelopes! Everyone was busy. No one had time for her or for friendship or for The Fabulous Five. It was awful. After all they had meant to each other. Now it seemed as if they didn't have anything in common anymore.

Well, I'll show them, she thought, and headed for her room. I'll change, too. After all, this is junior high! A plan was already beginning to form in her mind.

CHAPTER

3

*W*hen Melanie got to the media center the next morning, it was crowded with seventh-graders who wanted to help with the dance. She counted eleven girls, including herself, and nine boys. That ought to be plenty of kids, she thought with satisfaction. Enough to get the dance organized and enough to get her plan into action.

She had decided last night that the only way to get The Fabulous Five's attention was to become so popular and so busy with new friends that they couldn't help noticing. Then they would realize how much they missed her friendship, and they might even be a little bit jealous. Melanie smiled to herself and surveyed the crowd. Working on the seventh-grade dance was the perfect place to start.

There were several cute boys, including Derek Travelstead. He had dark brown hair, and he had the neatest freckles she had ever seen sprinkled across his face. When he smiled, he looked just like Kirk Cameron.

She also noticed Scott Daly and Shane Arrington standing together. Scott had been her boyfriend in sixth grade, and she still liked him and went out with him sometimes. In fact, she loved to daydream about the night a few weeks ago when he had taken her home from Laura McCall's party and kissed her good-night. But she liked Shane, too. He was one of her new crushes now that she was at Wacko. Her heart fluttered as she wondered if Scott and Shane could possibly be talking about her.

Jana and Randy and Christie and Jon were talking quietly together. Jana and Christie were the only other members of The Fabulous Five there besides herself, and she looked away quickly before they saw her and noticed that she was looking at them. They might think she was jealous that they were with boys and she wasn't.

She was just about to call out to Alexis Duvall and Jill Weinberg when Curtis Trowbridge dragged a chair into the center of the room and climbed on it. He put fingers into the corners of his mouth, whistling loudly for attention.

"Okay, everybody. Grab a chair." He waited for everyone to find a seat and then continued, "Listen up. We don't have much time, so we have to get started."

"The first thing we need to do is get a dance chairperson," said Taffy Sinclair. She looked gorgeous, as usual, with her long blond hair falling softly over her shoulders.

"She just wants to be the one picked," grumbled Dekeisha Adams, who was sitting right behind Melanie.

Melanie frowned at Taffy. Rats! she thought. Why didn't I think of that? My friends couldn't help noticing if I were the chairperson and everybody had to report to me.

Just then Laura McCall spoke up. "I think we should *elect* a chairperson."

"I vote for Laura," called out Melissa McConnell.

That made Melanie even angrier.

Curtis called for quiet again as kids started talking among themselves about which girl should be chairperson. "As class president, I have decided to be dance chairperson," Curtis said, "and I have already made out a list of committees that we'll need. They are: music, decorations, refreshments, and publicity." He waved a sheet of paper in the air as he announced each committee. "I am going to put these sheets on the media center bulletin board, and I'd like for you to sign up for whichever committee you'd like to be on."

"What a hard choice," Melanie mumbled to Dekeisha. "They all sound like fun."

Dekeisha nodded as Curtis went on talking. "Since I'm the dance chairperson, I will attend all the committee meetings, which means that each committee will meet on a different night. Refreshments on Monday. Decorations on Tuesday. Music on Wednesday. And publicity on Thursday. Since this is Tuesday, the first meeting of the decorations committee will be here in the media center tonight at seven P.M. If anybody has any questions, see me."

Kids began talking among themselves, discussing which committee they wanted to join, but Curtis wasn't through talking. "The next thing we have to discuss is a theme for the dance."

"What about a fifties sock hop?" suggested Chandra Sharp.

"Naw," said Brad Eisenhauer. "The eighth-graders had one last year. Let's do something different."

"I know!" shouted Joel Murphy, waving his hands in the air. "I have the *perfect* idea. Let's have a monster party."

Several girls made faces and a few boys groaned, but Joel wasn't finished.

"Come on, guys," he insisted. "Listen to this. Everyone could dress up as something weird. There are all kinds of monsters. And we could use that old song 'Monster Mash' for our theme song. I think I know somebody who has the record."

"Wow!" Scott Daly and Steve Hernandez shouted in unison.

"We've even got the perfect person to be one of the chaperons, *Dracula!*" added Whitney Larkin.

"Terrific," said Jon Smith.

Even some of the girls were smiling and nodding.

Melanie thought about it. It could be fun, especially if she could find the perfect costume. Maybe she could be Elvira or some sort of strange creature from outer space. In fact, the more she thought about the idea, the better she liked it, except for one part. How would Mr. Dracovitch feel about being a chaperon at a monster dance?

When a vote was taken, the monster party passed. Someone suggested calling it Wacko Wonderland, and everybody liked that, too. As the meeting broke up, Melanie joined the group that was swarming around the bulletin board to sign up for committees.

"Which one are you going to be on, Melanie?" asked Alexis.

"I want publicity," said Dekeisha. "Sign up for that one."

Melanie shrugged. "I haven't decided yet." She hung back purposely. She would decide when she saw who was on each committee. If she was going to use this dance to help her impress the rest of The Fabulous Five, she had to plan very carefully.

When the crowd thinned enough for her to reach the sheet for the music committee, she saw Shane's name on top of the list. I'm definitely on that one, she thought with a smile. She added her name under the others': Joel Murphy, Jon Smith, Laura McCall, and Brad Eisenhauer.

The next list was for decorations. Naturally, Taffy Sinclair had signed up for that one. But so had Jill Weinberg, Chandra Sharp, and Alexis Duvall. Even though there was only one boy on that committee, it was Derek Travelstead. It might be fun getting to know him better as well as becoming better friends with Alexis, Chandra, and Jill.

Melanie couldn't resist signing up for refreshments. Her own mother made the world's best brownies. She knew she could talk her into baking some for the dance, which would make Melanie a big hit with everyone. Christie and Melissa had signed up for that committee, too, and so had Randy and Steve Hernandez.

That only left publicity. Maybe I should skip that one, Melanie thought. I'm already on three. Just then she caught sight of the list. Jana's name was at the top, but so was Scott's. She couldn't pass up a committee that Scott was on. Besides, it would be the only chance for Jana to see how popular she was . . . or at least how popular she was going to be. Whitney Larkin and Dekeisha were on that committee, too.

When Melanie finally left the media center, her mind was whirling. She had signed up for all four committees. She couldn't believe she had done a thing like that. It meant that in addition to going to cheerleading practice a few days after school, she would have to go to a meeting every single night of the week. But each committee was important in its own special way.

"Get set, Fabulous Five," she whispered under her breath. "Look out for your old friend, Melanie Edwards!"

CHAPTER

4

Shane caught up with Melanie in the hall on the way to biology class after lunch. "I've come . . . to bite . . . your *neck!*" he said in his best Dracula voice.

Even though his words made her shiver, Melanie couldn't help giving him a wide smile. "Whoever heard of a blond, blue-eyed Dracula?" she joked. "You're a fake."

"Oh, my dear, that's where you're wrong," he said with a sinister laugh. "Vampires come in all colors, shapes, and sizes. Why, for all I know, even Igor may be a vampire."

"Now that I could believe," Melanie answered, and

then flinched as Shane slugged her playfully on the arm.

"Seriously, though, where do you suppose Mr. Dracovitch got all the cows' eyes for our class to dissect?" Shane asked. He wasn't smiling now, but Melanie could detect a slight twinkle in his eyes. "Do you suppose he went out into a farmer's pasture at night when the moon was full? Do you think he sucked all the blood out of the cows and then popped out their eyeballs?"

"Shane!" Melanie cried. "Knock it off. That's disgusting."

His eyes widened and his voice dropped to a hoarse whisper. "And then he brought them here to Wacko and put them into the refrigerators in the cafeteria for safekeeping until time for his classes to dissect them."

"Shane, I'm warning you," said Melanie.

"But alas! Something went wrong! The cooks found those eyeballs and ground them up and made them into meat loaf *and*"—he paused for dramatic effect—"served it for lunch today."

"Gross! Gross!" cried Melanie, but Shane was doubled over laughing. She ignored him, trying to keep her stomach from turning flip-flops. Why on earth had she gotten hot lunch today? she wondered. The meat loaf *wasn't* ground-up cows' eyeballs, of course, but thank goodness she had covered it with ketchup just the same.

She slipped into her seat in the biology lab, hoping that at least one of The Fabulous Five had seen her walking in the halls with Shane. That was part of her plan. Pretty soon they would realize that since they didn't need her anymore, she didn't need them either. She had plenty of friends—especially cute boys like Shane. But even if The Fabulous Five hadn't seen them together, Tammy Lucero certainly had. She was glaring at them as they entered the classroom, and Melanie knew she would run straight to Laura with the news.

Mr. Dracovitch was calling the class to attention and taking roll. Melanie tapped her pencil absently as he launched into a long list of instructions for the dissection. She could get all that later. Right now her thoughts were on Mr. Dracovitch and the seventh-grade dance. At the meeting this morning she had wondered how he might feel about being the honorary chaperon, and seeing him now, she wondered the same thing all over again. Did he realize how weird that shiny, black toupee made him look or know that kids called him Dracula behind his back? Would he think it was a pretty funny joke? Or would his feelings be hurt?

"All right now, class," he was saying. "It's time to take your places at the dissecting tables. Find your partners and choose a table."

Forgetting about the dance, Melanie scrambled out of her seat and made a beeline for the dissecting tables, almost stumbling over Whitney Larkin in the process. Shane sat nearer to them and was ahead of her, motioning back over his shoulder for her to follow him to a table at the back of the room. Fantastic! she thought. It was so much more private back there.

"Hi, Shane," she said brightly. "Are you ready for this?"

Shane nodded, rubbing his hands together and licking his lips as if in anticipation of a feast. "I've come to drink your blood," he said, arching his eyebrows at her.

"Shane! Cut it out!" she insisted, trying not to let it show that she loved his teasing.

It took forever for the whole class to get settled at tables. Melanie noticed with dismay that almost no one chose tables at the front of the room; everyone seemed to want to get as far away from Mr. Dracovitch's desk as possible. Shane's and her table wasn't going to be as private as she thought. Also, Tammy and Chandra's table was almost close enough to overhear their conversation.

"You will find a pan on your table," Mr. Dracovitch began in a tone that made the last few whisperers shut up.

Melanie glanced at the table. Sure enough, there was a small metal pan in the center. There was also a drain, a spigot, which she guessed was for water, and a gas jet. She shivered. This is getting serious, she thought. I'd better pay attention.

"Each pan has a number on it."

Shane looked the pan over and pointed to the number seven on the side. Melanie nodded, thinking that seven was always a lucky number. Being Shane's partner was meant to be.

"Remember that number," Mr. Dracovitch went on. "When you receive your specimen, it will go into the pan, and each day you will get your own team's pan from the refrigerator and resume working on it. Any questions?"

"What's that awful smell?" asked Shawnie Pendergast.

Melanie had smelled it, too, and she agreed with Shawnie that it was pretty awful.

Bill Soliday piped up, "Cows' eyes, what else?"

Laughter broke out in the room, but Mr. Dracovitch held up his hand for silence. "What you smell is formaldehyde," he said patiently. "It is a preservative. Actually, I find the odor rather pleasant, myself."

Next Mr. Dracovitch walked among the tables carrying a large metal bowl. Stopping at each table, he used a pair of tongs to extract a large, round object and drop it in the pan. Melanie closed her eyes. The closer he got to her table the more she knew she didn't want to look at the awful thing, much less touch it. If she could just get Shane to . . .

THUD!

She opened her eyes without meaning to. There in the pan was an enormous eye. It was wet and slimy looking, and it was staring straight at her. The room started to spin. She reached out to grab the table, but she felt arms close around her instead. She looked up into Shane's face.

"Are you okay?" he asked, holding on to her tightly.

"I think so," she said. "It's just so . . ."

Shane was nodding. "Gross," he said, finishing her sentence. "I think so, too, but we'll get used to it."

Melanie smiled gratefully. The room had stopped spinning now, and she noticed Mr. Dracovitch standing beside Shane looking awfully worried.

"Are you sure you're all right?" he asked. "Maybe you'd like to sit down or step out into the hall for some air."

"I'm fine," she insisted, and then smiled at Shane, who had moved back to his side of the table now. She couldn't believe how quickly he had rushed to take care of her. And what was just as super, Tammy Lucero had seen it all.

CHAPTER

5

*W*ith Shane's help Melanie managed to get through the rest of biology class. She made herself look at the specimen, as Mr. Dracovitch had called it, which was almost as big as a baseball. The white part and the pupil looked like any other eye, only bigger, but the rest of it was covered with a sort of bluish-black gel. "Gross," she whispered over and over again, and she could hear other kids reacting the same way.

All that the class was supposed to do the first day was weigh and measure the eyeball, which fortunately Shane did for both of them. He even wrote the results in both of their notebooks and whisked pan number seven into the refrigerator and out of her sight.

When the bell rang, Shane was out of the classroom door ahead of her, and she hurried to catch up.

"Thanks a million," she said. "A *zillion*, actually. Igor would have been proud of you."

The mention of Igor always made Shane's face light up. "Do you really think so?" he asked, flashing a big smile and slowing to walk beside her.

That was just what Melanie had planned. "Why don't you ask him?" she said. Crossing her fingers behind her back, she went on with the rest of her plan. "By the way, did you write down all of Dracula's instructions? You know, the stuff he was saying at the beginning of class."

Shane nodded.

"Great," she said, beaming her best smile straight at him. "I missed some of it, and I really want to get a good grade in this class. Especially since I embarrassed myself in front of Mr. Dracovitch by almost fainting." She paused a moment and lowered her eyes, hoping that he would remember putting his arm around her and rescuing her. "Anyway, do you think I could look at your notes and copy the parts I missed?"

"Sure," he said, opening his notebook to the section marked BIOLOGY. "You can take them with you and give them back to me later."

"I can't do that," Melanie insisted. "What I mean is that I have class the rest of the afternoon and won't

have time to copy them. What if I get them after school
. . . say at Bumpers? You'll be there, won't you?"

Melanie held her breath. This had to work. It just
had to.

"Okay," he said. "I'll see you at Bumpers. Bye."

Shane peeled off in the direction of his next class,
leaving Melanie feeling weak-kneed with relief. *Of
course* The Fabulous Five would be at Bumpers after
school. And *of course* they would see her with Shane.
So what if they don't have time for me anymore, she
thought. I don't have time for them anymore, either.
That's life. No, she corrected herself. That's junior
high.

After school, everything went just the way she had
planned. She sauntered into Bumpers, trying to look
totally casual. Out of the corner of one eye she could
see Beth and Katie sitting at a table. They had spotted
her, too, and Katie was waving in her direction.

"They probably just want me to come over to their
table so that they can have someone to ignore,"
Melanie grumbled under her breath.

Shane also spotted her just then. "Hey, Melanie," he
called out. "Come on over."

Even though Bumpers was noisy, Shane had
shouted so loud that Melanie was sure her friends had
heard.

Shane was sitting with four other boys from the seventh-grade football team: Tony Sanchez, Keith Masterson, Bill Kingman, and Randy Kirwan, and he was

telling them about the cow's-eyeball project when she walked up.

". . . and then old Dracula gets this big bowl of eyeballs out of the fridge and starts plopping them into the pans on everybody's table, and when he gets to our table . . . hey, Mel. Tell them what happened when he got to our table."

Melanie felt herself blushing. "It was gross," she said with a nervous laugh. "Let's change the subject, okay? We could talk about the seventh-grade dance."

"Sure," said Shane, looking apologetic, but the other guys wanted to hear more about the cow's eyeball.

"Come on, Melanie. Tell us what happened in biology class," said Keith.

"You can talk about it," insisted Tony. "It's all over with now."

Suddenly Melanie realized that she had their complete attention. She glanced quickly toward The Fabulous Five's table to make sure they had all noticed that she was in the spotlight with five gorgeous football players, but Beth and Katie were still by themselves. Where were Jana and Christie? she wondered. Then she spotted Christie and Jon at the order counter. Well, anyway Beth and Katie had noticed her. And so had a lot of other kids sitting around at nearby tables. Laura McCall and her three friends were glaring in her direction. Taffy Sinclair and Mona Vaughn had actually gotten up from their table and were standing close enough to hear.

"Well," she began, feeling like a movie star giving her first live television interview, "as Shane said, Dracula just plopped that great big *gruesome* eyeball into the pan on our table. It was actually *staring* at me!" Melanie added for effect.

"*Yew!*" cried Mona.

"Did you throw up?" asked Bill Kingman.

"No, silly," said Melanie. "I just . . ."

"Well, I almost did," interrupted Shawnie Pendergast. Melanie hadn't even noticed that she was nearby, but Shawnie immediately began telling everybody how she had had to run out of the room the day the project was announced.

Gradually the crowd around the table got bigger as more and more kids heard bits and pieces of the conversation and came over to listen. Shane and she talked the most, telling in great detail about the bluish-black gel on the backs of the eyeballs and the sickening smell of formaldehyde that hung in the air and about Dracula's standing over them in his black, shiny toupee.

Melanie tried to keep tabs on each of The Fabulous Five, but she missed seeing when any of them left. Still, it had been a wonderful afternoon. She felt more popular than she ever had in her life. Kids were crowding around her, clamoring to ask questions and hanging on to every word she said. And it wasn't until after Shane had walked her home and said good-bye that she remembered she had forgotten to borrow his notebook and copy his notes.

CHAPTER

6

It was midnight before Melanie finally finished her homework and switched off her bedside lamp. She was beat. The meeting of the decorations committee had been fun, especially since Derek Travelstead had paid a lot of attention to her, but it had lasted far longer than she had expected. That was mainly because Taffy Sinclair had had so many crazy ideas—such as decorating in pastel colors. Melanie closed her eyes to go to sleep, but she could still see Taffy's face and hear her voice as she argued her point.

"Just because the dance theme is 'Wacko Wonderland' and everyone is coming dressed as a monster doesn't mean that the decorations have to be black and orange like Halloween," she had insisted. "If kids used their imaginations, they could come up with some really *neat* monsters instead of the same old thing."

"Hey, I was picturing bats and spiders and stuff like that dangling from the ceiling," said Derek Travelstead, grinning at Melanie and then winking.

"Me, too," said Jill Weinberg. "Whoever heard of pastel monsters?"

"Did you see *Ghostbusters?*" Taffy challenged. "The monster in that may not have been pastel, but it was white."

The argument had gone on and on, with Melanie reminding everybody of Shane's green and purple and yellow dinosaur for the parent project. Curtis mentioned that Alf was orange, and someone else said that Alf was an alien from another planet and not a monster. Then the subject had switched to Mr. Dracovitch.

"I suppose that if we all come as pastel monsters, someone will have to talk Dracula into showing up in a blond wig instead of his regular black one," offered Chandra.

Alexis had laughed like crazy. "It certainly might help his image," she said.

The meeting had finally broken up without any real decisions made. Everybody had agreed to think things over before the meeting next Tuesday.

Chuckling to herself, Melanie turned over to go to sleep, wondering if her dreams would be filled with pastel monsters.

* * *

Jana was standing alone at The Fabulous Five's spot by the fence the next morning when Melanie got to school. She had wondered where Jana was at Bumpers the day before and if she had seen the way Shane and she had entertained the crowd with stories about Dracula and the eyeball project.

She was debating whether or not to join Jana at the fence when Garrett Boldt came loping toward her, his camera swinging from the strap over his shoulder. Garrett was an eighth-grader and sports photographer for the yearbook, and he was totally gorgeous. He was also one of the boys Melanie had a crush on.

"Hey, Melanie. How's it going?"

"Hey, yourself," she shot back, and gave him her most dazzling smile. "Everything's great."

He fell into step beside her. "That was one funny story you and Shane told at Bumpers yesterday. Leave it to old Dracula to come up with something new this year. When I took biology last year, all we got to dissect was your standard frog."

"Frogs. Eyeballs. If you ask me, they're all gross," Melanie admitted.

Garrett stopped and looked thoughtful. "You know," he began, "you should talk to Jana and Funny about getting some pictures of you guys working on your eyeballs for the seventh-grade section of *The Wigwam*. It would be a riot."

Melanie cast a sidelong glance toward Jana. "Terrific

idea," she said, wondering why she hadn't thought of it herself. "I'd better go talk to Jana about it right now," she added.

Garrett went off toward some friends, and Melanie headed for the fence where Jana stood. This time it was Dekeisha Adams and Mandy McDermott who stopped her.

"I can't stop laughing about you guys and your cows' eyeballs," said Mandy, immediately breaking into a fit of giggles.

"Me, either," said Dekeisha. "That's the funniest story I ever heard. I almost wish I was in that class."

"Not me!" insisted Mandy. "I'd die if I had to touch one of those things."

Then Dekeisha began talking about the dance and how glad she was that she was on the publicity committee with Melanie, so that by the time Melanie was able to get away from them, the first bell was ringing. And when she looked toward the spot by the fence, Jana was already gone. As upset as she was at The Fabulous Five for practically snubbing her lately, she couldn't help feeling a little bit disappointed that she had to walk to the lockers alone. It seemed strange not to be doing everything together. Oh, well, she thought with a sigh, I'll get a chance to talk to them in the cafeteria at lunch. I can ask Jana then about taking the biology-class picture for the yearbook.

All through her morning classes Melanie kept thinking about her friends. Maybe she had been wrong to believe they weren't interested in her anymore. Maybe they even thought *she* was snubbing them. Still, she reasoned, no matter what subject she had tried to bring up lately, they all seemed to want to talk about something else. And The Fabulous Five hadn't been spending much time together these days, either. It was as if they were all starting to go their own separate ways. The stories she had heard must be true. This was the way it was supposed to be in junior high.

When the lunch bell rang, she pushed her way through the crowded halls toward the cafeteria. She had made up her mind to give them one last chance. She would sit with her friends and act as if nothing were wrong between them.

"Hi, gang," she said, plopping her lunch bag down on the table. Christie and Jana were already there, and they both looked up and returned her greeting. Katie and Beth had come in behind her, and Melanie waited patiently for everyone to get settled at the table before she began her story about biology class.

"Wait until I tell you guys what old Dracula is making us dissect in biology class," she began.

"A cow's eyeball," said Katie. "We heard all about it from Shawnie Pendergast."

"Oh," said Melanie, feeling deflated. "Well, it's really a gross thing to look at, all bluish-black and yucky."

"Do we have to talk about it at lunch?" asked Christie. She faked sticking her finger down her throat to throw up and rolled her eyes at Melanie.

"I agree," said Jana. "It's disgusting."

Melanie shrugged and took a bite of her tuna sandwich. It tasted like cardboard. So what if cows' eyeballs were disgusting? she thought. It would still make a funny picture for the yearbook. She sighed and then remembered the seventh-grade dance. Surely they would want to talk about that.

She started to speak and then stopped. Around the table conversation was starting again. Katie was telling Jana about a case that had come before Teen Court the week before. Christie and Beth were discussing a math assignment. But no one was saying a word to her. They were ignoring her. Acting as if she weren't even there. Plus, no one had even mentioned her invitation to sleep over Saturday night after they had all acted so sad when they turned her down. It was as if she didn't exist anymore.

Melanie looked down at her sandwich. She had only taken one bite, but one bite was enough. There was no way she could eat any more of it. She gathered up her belongings and glanced around the table one more time before standing up to leave. Her old friends were still deep in their own conversations. No one would even notice when she was gone.

This is junior high, she reminded herself. Friendships change. It's going to be *fun* being friends with Mandy and Dekeisha and Alexis and Jill and all the others. And she hurried away to look for her new friends.

CHAPTER

7

When Melanie left the cafeteria, the first person she saw was Funny Hawthorne.

"Hi, Melanie," Funny called out in her usual bubbly way as they passed in the hall.

"Hi, Funny," said Melanie. She whirled around and reached out to stop Funny. "By the way, have you heard about Dracula's biology project yet?"

"Sure," said Funny. "It's all over school. What a scream."

"Have you thought about getting some pictures of kids working on their eyeballs for the seventh-grade section of the yearbook?"

"Wow! What a terrific idea," cried Funny. "What time do you have the class?"

"First period after lunch."

"Excellent. I have study hall then. I'll get a camera from the yearbook staff room and see if I can get permission to come into the class and shoot pictures. I'd better run if I'm going to get all that done before the bell rings."

Funny took off down the hall and then skidded to a stop. "Melanie," she called over her shoulder, "thanks a million for the idea."

Melanie nodded and watched with mixed feelings as Funny raced toward the yearbook staff room. She really should have told Jana. After all, they had been best friends for ages. But another part of her was glad that she had told Funny instead.

She wandered out of the building and sat down on the front steps. She had remembered to borrow Shane's biology notes in English class this morning, and this was a good time to copy them. She certainly wouldn't have time to do it tonight because the music committee was having its first meeting and Miss Dickinson had given a huge reading assignment in English. She would probably be up late again tonight. Just thinking about it made her tired.

She yawned and shook the cobwebs from her head, trying to focus on copying the biology notes. Instead, her mind wandered. Why did things always have to get so complicated? she wondered. If her friends hadn't started snubbing her in the first place, she wouldn't have to work so hard to make new friends. She sat there for a long time staring off into space and thinking about the situation with her friends. Sometimes she felt like crying when she thought about the great times they had had together. No matter how she tried to fake it, making new friends would never be the same.

The bell rang, interrupting her thoughts. She still hadn't finished copying Shane's biology notes and it was time for class. Maybe she could borrow them again later.

When she got to the biology room, Funny was waiting for her, standing beside the row of cages where Mr. Dracovitch kept his menagerie, and wearing her usual big smile. There was a camera in her hand.

When Melanie walked up, Funny pointed to the cages and asked, "You don't have to dissect any of these, do you?"

Melanie chuckled. "No. They're just his pets. The two crows are Heckle and Jeckle, after the cartoon crows, and the snake is named Sirloin Snake. Isn't that hysterical?"

Funny nodded. "It's all set up," she said. "Mr. Dracovitch was really nice about letting me take pictures during the class." Looking toward the teacher, she covered her mouth with her hand and whispered, "Does he know yet that he gets to be a chaperon for our monster dance?"

Melanie shrugged. "I don't know. I guess it's up to Curtis to invite him. He's the dance chairman."

"Mr. Dracovitch will be perfect," said Funny.

"Clarence Marshall *swears* that he brings formaldehyde instead of coffee in his thermos."

"Oh, come on," said Melanie. "That's silly. Besides, how would Clarence know a thing like that?"

"Do you remember when Clarence had to be hall monitor for a week when Teen Court found him guilty of fighting with Tony Calcaterra?"

Melanie nodded.

"Well, according to Clarence, he had to take a phone message to someone in the teachers' lounge, and he saw Dracula pour formaldehyde out of the thermos, into a cup, and then take a drink. He said he knew it was formaldehyde because he could smell it all the way across the room."

"All right, class," called Mr. Dracovitch suddenly. "Time to take your seats and get started."

Melanie drifted to her seat, feeling strange about what Funny had just told her. Clarence Marshall wasn't the most trustworthy person in the world, of course. But Mr. Dracovitch was a little weird. Surely he realized that his toupee made him look exactly like Dracula. Was there some reason he wore such a black, shiny one and pulled it so far down on his forehead? Why couldn't he wear a brown, curly wig? Or a blond one? And hadn't he said the first day of the experiment that he liked the smell of formaldehyde? Was it possible that he liked it well enough to drink it?

When everyone was seated, Mr. Dracovitch started talking about how the eye worked. He discussed the pupil and the lens and the retina and then said the class was ready to begin dissecting their cows' eyeballs to see what all these parts looked like.

When they got to the dissecting tables, Mr. Dracovitch allowed Funny to wander around, taking pictures of first one team and then another. Shane crossed his eyes and stuck out his tongue, hamming it up and pretending he was dying when she stopped at their table.

"Cut it out, Shane," Melanie whispered. "Don't you want her to choose our picture for the yearbook?"

Shane gave her a surprised look. "Yeah, you're right," he said. He picked up the big, bluish-black eyeball and held it high.

"Grab on," he instructed Melanie. "Then we'll give her our toothiest grins. She'll never be able to pass up a photo like that."

"You've got to be kidding," Melanie muttered. She hadn't meant for him to carry things that far.

"Think of the publicity," said Shane. "And hurry up. Formaldehyde is running down my arm."

Melanie shook her head at Shane in wonder, but she had to admit it would be good publicity. She could certainly use every bit she could get. She took a deep breath and slowly reached for the eyeball, being careful not to look at it. She flinched slightly when her fingers touched the slimy thing, but she held the pose and smiled her best at Funny as the camera flashed.

CHAPTER

8

*M*elanie was fifteen minutes late arriving for the
music committee meeting. She had been hurrying as
fast as she could ever since she got home from school,
but there was just simply too much to do and too little
time now that she was attending dance committee
meetings every single night of the week.

She pushed open the media center door and eased in
quietly. Shane, Joel Murphy, Laura McCall, Brad
Eisenhauer, and Jon Smith were seated at a library
table listening to Curtis, who had the floor.

"We aren't going to have much money to work

with," Curtis was saying. He paused when he noticed Melanie enter the room.

She looked toward the table and was surprised to see Shane motioning her to an empty chair on his left. It was all that Melanie could do to keep from shooting a triumphant look in Laura's direction as she ducked across the room and dropped into the chair.

"We can't really afford a band," Curtis went on once she was seated.

"What about a disc jockey from one of the local stations to play records?" asked Laura. She looked at Shane the whole time she was talking, and Melanie knew she was trying to get his attention.

Jon Smith shook his head. "They're expensive, too. Maybe we could get somebody from our own class to be the disc jockey."

Melanie's face lit up and her hand shot into the air as she got a brilliant idea. "How about Shane?" she shouted. "He has tons of albums and tapes, and he'd do a *great job*."

For an instant she felt embarrassed about her outburst. Everybody was looking at her, including Shane. They probably thought she had flipped out. And what if he didn't want to do it? Or what if the committee thought it was a dumb idea?

Then Brad Eisenhauer shouted out, "Yeah. Shane would be terrific."

"Would you do it?" Curtis asked Shane, and Melanie held her breath, praying that he would say yes.

Shane didn't say anything for a moment. He seemed to be thinking it over. Finally a slow smile spread over his face, and he looked around the table and said, "Only if my assistant can come along."

"Your assistant?" Curtis said, puzzled.

"Sure," said Shane. "Igor, who else?"

The whole committee broke up over that, and it took Curtis forever to get everyone settled down so that he could take a vote.

When the meeting broke up and they were heading for the door, Melanie saw Laura watching her and Shane out of the corner of her eye as they walked out together. He hadn't paid the slightest attention to Laura all during the meeting, and now he turned to Melanie and said, "Do you realize that you may have just started me on a lifetime career as a disc jockey?"

Melanie laughed. "You and Igor. Are you serious about bringing him to the dance as your assistant? What can he do?"

Shane faked looking hurt. "You underestimate him. Igor can do lots of things."

"Like what?"

"Well, he can change the records and tapes, for one thing," Shane insisted. "And pick out what to play next."

"*Suuuure* he can," Melanie said slyly.

"Speaking of picking out the music," Shane said when they reached the media center door, "why don't I come over to your house Friday night and bring my albums? We can look through them and pick out what to play for the dance."

Melanie's heart missed a beat. "Do you mean just the two of us? Without the rest of the committee?"

"Sure." Then he added with a grin, "Unless you want me to bring Igor."

"I'm sure he would pick out some great tunes," she joked, "but I think we can get along without him this time."

Melanie was amazed to see that it was already ten o'clock when she and Shane said good-bye, and she hurried to the school's pay phone to call her father to pick her up from the meeting. She dialed and then rubbed her eyes sleepily as she waited for someone to answer the phone. How had it gotten so late so fast? she wondered. She still had Shane's biology notes to copy and fifteen pages to read for English Lit. She also wanted to wash out her new pink shirt to wear tomorrow. She would be absolutely dead when it came time to get up in the morning.

She did manage to wash out her shirt and copy Shane's notes, but when she tried to read, the words blurred together. Finally she decided to set her alarm for half an hour earlier than usual so that she could finish her reading assignment in the morning.

When the alarm went off, it was still dark outside, and Melanie couldn't believe that it was time to get up already. She sat up and checked her clock and then fell back against the pillow in disgust. It was morning, after all, and she was totally exhausted. How could she possibly do her reading assignment when her eyes refused to open? Maybe she could rest for just a few more minutes. . . .

She woke up to the sound of the telephone ringing. Sun was streaming in her window.

"Oh, my gosh!" she yelped, jumping straight up in bed.

The clock on her bedside table said 9:37, and the sound of the telephone pierced the air like a siren.

She had gone back to sleep! And no one in her family had bothered to wake her! Where was everybody? Why didn't her mother or Jeffy answer the phone?

She sailed out of bed and ran for the phone, grabbing the receiver just as it rang for the umpteenth time. She was so out of breath she could barely say hello.

"Good morning," a woman said crisply. "This is the Wakeman Junior High attendance office. Am I speaking to Mrs. Edwards?"

Melanie was thunderstruck. All she could do for a moment was stare at the phone and listen to her heart pound. *The Wakeman Junior High attendance office?* They were checking up on her. Calling to ask why she wasn't in school and why her mother hadn't called the attendance office to report the absence before nine o'clock the way she was supposed to. *I can't fake it,* she thought. *She'll know I'm not my mother.*

"No," she answered. "This is Melanie. I think my mother must have gone out early and forgotten to wake me. I'll get there as soon as I can . . . if that's okay."

There was a pause on the other end of the line and then a sigh, and finally the woman replied, "All right. We'll let it go this time."

Melanie ducked into the kitchen to pour herself a glass of milk and look for a note from her mother. She found the note in the middle of the kitchen table. It was just as she had thought. Her mother and little brother had left early and would be gone for the day. Of course she didn't wake me, Melanie reasoned, I always set my alarm.

Oh, brother, she thought as she raced to her room to get ready for school. I hope the rest of the day isn't going to be like this.

CHAPTER

9

*E*ven though Melanie rushed, by the time she had showered, washed and blow-dried her hair, and dressed, it was lunch period at school. In her hurry to get out of the house she had forgotten to fix herself a lunch.

"I'm famished," she mumbled as she entered the cafeteria where the smell of sloppy joes rose from the steam tables. Even though it was anyone's guess what they were made from, it was generally agreed that sloppy joes were the best of what the Wacko cafeteria had to offer.

"Rats!" she said twice as loud, pulling a handful of

52

change out of her purse. "I don't have enough money for hot lunch." Sighing, she got potato chips out of the snack machine and surveyed the crowded lunchroom for someone to sit with.

Beth was alone at the table where The Fabulous Five usually sat together. She was munching away on an apple and writing something in her notebook. Should I go over and sit with her and act as if everything is normal between us? Melanie wondered. If she looks over at me and waves, it would be okay, she decided. Otherwise . . . maybe not. It would be too embarrassing if I go over on my own and she doesn't even say hello.

Melanie glanced around some more. Christie was on the other side of the cafeteria sitting with Jon. They were laughing and talking together as if there were no one else in the room. Jana and Funny sat together in the far corner. There wasn't much doubt what they were talking about: the yearbook. That seemed to be all Jana could think about anymore. Katie was nowhere to be seen, but Melanie supposed she was with some of her fellow judges on Teen Court. They're probably discussing a case, she thought. She stood by the snack machine for a moment feeling depressed and trying to decide what to do. She had to bite her lip to keep it from quivering.

She stole quick glances toward each of The Fabulous Five. She didn't want them to see her looking and think she was begging to sit with them, but she didn't want to miss it if one of them saw her and motioned for her to come over.

"Hi, Melanie. Where have you been? Did you hear the big news yet?" Sara Sawyer had approached her and looked as if she were about to burst.

"Gosh, no," said Melanie. "I overslept and just got to school. What happened?"

"Sirloin is missing. Everybody's scared to death."

Melanie squinted at Sara and asked in a puzzled voice, "Sirloin is missing? What are you talking about?"

"You know. Dracula's pet, Sirloin Snake. He's missing from his cage in the biology room, and wait until you hear all the rumors that are flying around."

Melanie's scalp prickled at the thought of a snake loose in the school. "What kind of rumors?"

"You know how kids joke about Mr. Dracovitch's being Dracula?" Sara began, and Melanie nodded. "Well, now they're saying all kinds of crazy things. For instance, Dracula bit Sirloin, turning him into a vampire, and then turned him loose in the school to make vampires out of all the kids."

"You're kidding," said Melanie. "Nobody would believe a thing like that. Calling Mr. Dracovitch Dracula is just a joke."

"Sure, it's a joke, but nobody's taking any chances. Half the kids in my morning classes sat with their feet up in their chairs. Mr. Naset ordered everybody in our history class to put their feet on the floor, but nobody budged. Joel Murphy even yelled out, 'I'm not going to be turned into a vampire! No way!' and everybody in the class applauded."

"Wow!" said Melanie, automatically looking toward the floor for anything that might be slithering around her own feet. She didn't really believe that her biology teacher was a vampire, but she had to admit that she didn't want to take any chances either. "What does Mr. Dracovitch say happened to Sirloin?" she asked.

Sara shrugged. "Just that one of the hinges on the door to his cage broke or fell off or something and that Sirloin got out on his own. He also says that snakes are mostly nocturnal and that Sirloin is probably curled up in a dark corner somewhere sleeping until night-time. He *says* that nobody has anything to worry about because Sirloin is a common garden snake and won't bite unless he's threatened, and that even if he did bite, he isn't poisonous. But I don't know. A snake is a snake, if you ask me."

"And a vampire is a vampire," said Alexis, who had come up while Sara was talking.

"So, what's going to happen?" asked Melanie. "I mean, is anybody looking for it? Did anybody form a snake patrol, or anything? I can't believe they didn't call off school."

Alexis shook her head. "Mr. Bell came over the loud-speaker during first period and instructed everybody to stay calm."

"He also said that if anybody saw the snake they were to leave it alone and tell a teacher immediately," said Sara.

"Well, I'll tell you one thing," growled Alexis. "I'm

not going *anywhere* alone. Not to the rest room. Not to my locker. Not anywhere! Not until that snake is found."

Melanie's eyes widened as she thought about opening her locker and finding a snake inside. Still, she reasoned, there was no way for it to get into her locker. The door was locked, and snakes were too big to slip through any of the vents. She shuddered. All the same, she agreed with Alexis. She wouldn't go to her locker alone until the snake was found. Eeek! she thought an instant later. I have biology next period, and I need to go to my locker to get my book.

"Speaking of lockers, anybody interested in walking with me to *my* locker?" she asked.

"Sorry," said Alexis. "I've got to talk to Lisa Snow."

"Can't," said Sara. "I was supposed to be in the media center five minutes ago to look up some history stuff with Stacy Holgrem."

Melanie glanced at her watch as the others smiled apologetically and left. "Great. Just great," she muttered. It was less than five minutes until time for the bell. She hadn't even eaten a single potato chip yet, and she was starving. Worst of all, she needed to go to her locker, and there just might be a vampire snake curled up inside waiting to jump out and bite her. So much for my day's getting any better, she thought.

CHAPTER

10

*J*ust then Melanie spotted Scott. He was leaving the cafeteria, sauntering nonchalantly out the door, and he wasn't carrying any books. He had to be heading for his locker.

Melanie put on a burst of speed, rushing through the crowded cafeteria to catch him. She had to skid to a stop, turn sideways, and suck in her breath to avoid a collision with Eric Silverman, who was carrying his dishes to the tray return, but when she stepped into the hall, Scott was still in sight.

"Scott! Wait up!" she shouted. Arriving beside him

out of breath, she smiled quickly and went on. "You're on your way to your locker, right?"

"You've got it," said Scott. "I suppose you want to go along, and then you want me to protect you if Sirloin Snake is in yours."

"You've got it," Melanie echoed, and then burst out laughing. "I know he isn't, of course. But just the same . . ."

They fell into step together and made casual conversation as they walked along. Being with Scott always made her feel happy, and she knew it showed in her voice.

As they reached her locker, she paused and looked at him thoughtfully. "You know," she began, "I keep thinking about Mr. Dracovitch."

"You mean that he's a vampire?" Scott asked.

"Yes. I mean no. That's just it. He isn't a vampire. Not really. And everybody knows that. But the way kids keep joking about it, it's bound to get back to him pretty soon. I wonder how he'll feel?"

Scott nodded. "I've been thinking about that, too. Especially since everybody wants to make him a chaperon for the monster dance. That plus all this business about a vampire snake on the loose in Wacko Junior High could really shake him up if he ever found out."

Melanie nodded. As Scott waited, she pulled open her locker and checked inside. No snake, she thought with relief. She grabbed her book, and then headed toward the biology classroom door. Out of the corner of her eye she could see Tammy Lucero staring in

Scott's and her direction. She's so nosy, thought Melanie. She's probably dying to know what we were talking about.

After Scott went off to his class, Melanie sank down into her seat and thought about Mr. Dracovitch. Even though she was nervous about a snake on the loose in the school, she felt sorry for her teacher. He's really nice, she thought, and kids aren't being fair to him. She wished she could talk to her friends about it, but they probably wouldn't listen, even if she brought it up. They hadn't heard anything she had said for days.

As soon as class began, it was obvious to Melanie that Mr. Dracovitch was worried. His face was whiter than usual, and his toupee seemed to be slightly at an angle, as if he had been mopping his forehead and accidentally knocked it askew.

"I want to emphasize that Sirloin is harmless," he began in a low, monotone voice. "He's used to people, and you students all know that he sleeps during the day. So just try not to be alarmed. We will find the snake and get him back into his cage, and nobody will get hurt."

Melanie felt sorrier for him than ever. What would happen if they didn't find the snake? Would he lose his job? She noticed that in spite of Mr. Dracovitch's reassurances most kids sat with their feet tucked under them, safely off the floor.

Instead of sending the class to the dissecting tables to work on the specimens, Mr. Dracovitch assigned two chapters in the text to be read during class. Then, as they opened their books and began reading, he paced up and down in front of the blackboard deep in thought.

Melanie rested her chin in her hand and tried to read, but her eyes wanted to close. Even after over-sleeping this morning, she was still exhausted. The publicity committee for the dance would meet tonight, too. There was cheerleading practice after school, and then there would be homework. *And she still hadn't eaten anything all day!* As if on cue, her stomach growled, and she looked around quickly to be sure no one had heard. She didn't even know what had happened to the potato chips she had bought in the cafeteria. I must have dropped them somewhere when I ran to catch Scott, she thought.

The harder she tried to read the assignment, the more the words swam together. Her eyes simply re-fused to stay open, and every so often her head drooped, startling her and making her bolt straight up. Slowly the words on the page were replaced by dreamy pictures. Mr. Dracovitch dropping something into the pans on the dissecting tables. Were they eye-balls or were they snakes? She couldn't see them clearly enough to tell.

She was dreaming. She knew it, and she fought to wake up. Instead, the pictures changed. She was in Bumpers now, surrounded by girls. Katie. Beth. Christie. And Jana. They were all frowning at her and shaking their heads.

"We don't like you anymore," said Katie. "You never talk about anything *we* want to talk about."

"We don't want to be friends anymore," said Beth. "We've all made new friends."

"*Better* friends," said Christie.

"The Fabulous Five is through," said Jana.

Melanie tried to talk to them, but no words would come out. She tried to shout, but she couldn't make a sound. Finally, she reached out toward them and POOF! All four of them vanished into thin air.

Just then a high-pitched sound echoed in her mind. She opened her eyes and recognized the bell ringing to end the class. All around her, kids were scrambling for the door, but Melanie sat still for a while, unable to shake off the effects of the dream.

"What if it wasn't a dream?" she whispered, and then shuddered. "What if it was a premonition?"

CHAPTER

11

$\mathcal{M}$elanie was so tired that she had to drag herself to the publicity committee meeting after supper. She didn't dare miss it, though, because Dekeisha and Jana would both be there, and she wanted Jana to see how friendly Dekeisha was becoming toward her. There was another reason, too. Scott would be there. The only trouble was that she liked other boys, too, such as Shane and Garrett Boldt and now, maybe even Derek Travelstead.

Although she wasn't actually late this time, Melanie was the last committee member to reach the media center. Everyone sat around a large library table at the front of the room talking, and they looked up when she came in. She stopped cold when she realized that there was an empty chair beside both Jana and Dekeisha, who sat across the table from each other, and that each of them was looking at her expectantly. Now what? she wondered, scanning the room for a way out of her dilemma.

It was Dekeisha who made the decision for her. "Come on, Melanie. Sit by me," she called.

As Melanie sank gratefully into the chair beside Dekeisha, she couldn't help casting a sidelong glance at Jana. Jana had looked away, her face hidden now so that Melanie could not see her expression. Was she angry at Melanie for not sitting beside her? Was she glad? Or what? Melanie wondered. Maybe if she could just catch Jana's eye and smile or something, it would smooth things over. But Jana seemed determined not to look her way.

"Hey, I just thought of something," said Scott, jumping to his feet.

Scott absolutely loved to tease, and Melanie could tell by the impish grin on his face that he was up to something now. "Old Dracula says snakes are nocturnal. What if Sirloin wakes up from his nap and decides to come to our committee meeting?"

Dekeisha gasped and jumped onto her chair while everyone else scrambled to search the dimly lighted library floor.

Scott tramped around the room, holding his hand straight out above his eyes like the visor of a cap, and acted as if he were searching for the snake. When he reached the darkest corner, he stopped and shouted, "Tracks!"

This time Dekeisha screamed. Melanie threw Scott a look that said "knock it off" and pretended to be calm. She knew that Scott was only faking, but she couldn't help glancing around. To her great relief, no snake was in sight. She glanced at Jana, too, thinking maybe talk of the missing snake might make her join in the conversation. No such luck. She kept on looking away from the group.

"I think we'd better get started with the meeting," said Curtis. Everybody nodded and mumbled their agreement. Shrugging, Scott gave up on his joke and sat down, too.

Melanie forgot about Jana for the time being as Curtis talked about getting art supplies and making posters at the next meeting. That will be fun, thought Melanie. Just as Whitney Larkin was making a suggestion about what should go on the posters, something thunked against her notebook. It was a tightly folded piece of paper. A note, probably, she thought. She twisted around and looked behind Dekeisha. Scott was looking back. Then he grinned and motioned toward the note in her hand. She opened it quickly.

Melanie,
Let's walk home together after the meeting.
　　　　　　　　　　　　　　　　　　Scott

Melanie thought a moment and then nodded back to Scott. She was supposed to call her dad to pick her up, but surely he wouldn't mind if Scott walked her home tonight. Besides, she thought slyly, Jana could hardly miss seeing her leave the school with Scott, and *of course* she would tell the rest of The Fabulous Five.

Just as Melanie had predicted, Jana was standing by the front door when she and Scott went out. Melanie felt triumphant. Surely Jana would get on the phone to the rest of The Fabulous Five the moment she got home. They would have to start noticing how popular she was getting. It wouldn't be long before they realized that if they didn't need her, she certainly didn't need them.

Scott was unusually quiet on the walk home. He probably thinks I'm mad at him for teasing about the snake, she thought, smiling to herself. If my feelings are important to him, that means he really cares.

"That was a pretty funny joke you pulled on the publicity committee," she said, hoping that saying so would make him feel better.

"I thought things were starting out pretty dull," he said with a grin. "I decided to liven them up. I'm glad you aren't mad."

"You certainly did liven things up," Melanie said. "I really wish they'd find that snake, though. I know he's just a garden snake and not poisonous or a vampire or anything like that, but he's making everybody nervous."

"He's probably long gone by now," said Scott.

"What do you mean?"

"He probably found an open window and just slithered out. Or maybe he crawled into a garbage can in the cafeteria looking for something to eat and got thrown into the Dumpster. Lots of things could have happened. With Mr. Dracovitch and the rest of the teachers and *all* the kids looking for him, don't you think he would have been found if he was still around?"

"Maybe," Melanie conceded. She hoped he was right, but she didn't feel quite so confident.

When they reached her house, she smiled at Scott and said, "Thanks for walking home with me. I'm really excited about the dance, and I think it's going to be fun working on the publicity committee."

"Me, too," he said. Then, acting suddenly shy, he looked down at the ground and began drawing invisible circles with the toe of his sneaker.

What's wrong? she wondered, but before she could run through a list of possibilities, he looked up at her again and said, "Would you go to the dance with me?"

Melanie stared at him in surprise. She had been so busy with all the committees and with trying to impress The Fabulous Five with her popularity that she hadn't even thought about a date for the dance.

"Gosh! I'd love to!" she burst out.

"Great," he said. His momentary shyness seemed to disappear, and he moved closer to her. Then he put his arms around her and kissed her.

Melanie was walking on air when she went inside. Her life was just about as perfect as it could get. Not only had Scott asked her to the dance, he had kissed her! And she was making new friends and getting more popular every day. She paused when she got to her room and thought, Maybe I *don't* need The Fabulous Five anymore, after all.

CHAPTER

12

*W*hen Melanie woke up the next morning, her head ached and her throat was sore, but she hardly noticed. It had taken forever to go to sleep. She had lain awake instead, remembering Scott's good-night kiss over and over again. Then she had closed her eyes and, as she drifted off to sleep, imagined how

Melanie Edwards
+
Scott Daly

would look written in twinkling stars on the velvety black sky.

But now with harsh sunlight streaming in her window, all she could think about was the rush she was in. For the third night in a row she hadn't been able to finish her homework. If I don't take time to iron the outfit I had planned to wear today, thought Melanie, I could wear something else and maybe have time to finish the list of history questions before I leave for school.

The day went by in a haze. She felt as if she had weights tied to her arms and legs as she moved from class to class, and her headache refused to go away. Even though she sat with the rest of The Fabulous Five in the cafeteria at noon, she didn't have the energy to join in the conversation. Normally she would have told them about her date with Scott for the dance, and that Shane was coming over tonight to select the music, and Katie would have groaned and told her she was boy crazy again. Instead, she listened to their chatter about all the things they were doing and thought for the zillionth time that it seemed as though they were all going their own separate ways.

When Shane got to her house around seven o'clock that evening, Melanie was feeling better. After supper she had showered and taken a couple of aspirins for her headache. She wasn't going to let anything spoil an evening with Shane if she could help it.

"Wow! You really do have a lot of music," she said

when she opened the door and saw him standing there with a huge stack of albums in one arm and a cassette carrier in the other.

"You ain't seen nothin' yet," he assured her, setting the tape carrier inside the door. "If you can grab these albums, I'll get the rest out of the car."

Melanie took the albums and watched as Shane hurried out to the curb where an ancient orange Volkswagen bug with flowers and butterflies painted on the side sat idling. He pulled out another armload of albums and waved good-bye to his father, who drove away in a cloud of black exhaust and fumes.

Leave it to Shane's hippie parents to have a car like that, she thought, chuckling to herself.

Her mother had whipped up a batch of her famous brownies when she heard that Shane would be over, and Melanie proudly set them in the middle of the kitchen table and fixed glasses of soda while Shane hauled in all the albums and tapes and arranged them in neat stacks.

Just then Jeffy bounded into the kitchen and skidded to a stop beside Shane. He looked at the albums on the table and then asked in a high-pitched little voice, "Do you have a Wee Sing album?"

"Sorry, partner," Shane said, tousling Jeffy's reddish-brown hair. "No Wee Sing. I've got Brain Damage, though. Do you like them?"

"Bwain Damage! Bwain Damage!" Jeffy shouted, jumping up and down. "My sister was in their show!"

Melanie couldn't help smiling at her little brother.

She loved being reminded of the time during The Fabulous Five's bragging war with The Fantastic Foursome when she and her four best friends had been called up onto the stage during Brain Damage's concert to join the zany British rock group in a song. Would The Fabulous Five ever go to a concert together again? she wondered wistfully.

While she had been lost in thought, her parents had come into the kitchen to say hello to Shane and to coax Jeffy into the family room so that Melanie could entertain Shane in peace. Glancing at the plate, Melanie noticed that it had cost the largest brownie to get Jeffy out of the room, but it would be worth it.

Melanie shook her head at the mountains of music. "The dance is only four hours long, you know," she teased.

"Which means we have our work cut out for us," said Shane, reaching for a brownie. "So we'd better have some of these to keep our energy level up."

For the next hour and a half they chattered happily as they went through the albums and tapes, sorting them into piles of Yes, No, and Maybe. Then they went through the Maybe pile and divided them into Probably No, Probably Yes, and Maybe Maybe.

"I think we can definitely eliminate the Probably Nos and probably the Maybe Maybes," said Melanie.

"And maybe even the Probably Yeses," said Shane. "After all, as you said, the dance is only four hours long."

Melanie frowned. "But there is some awfully good

music in the Probably Yes pile. Maybe we could put it on the bottom of the Definitely Yes stack, just in case you have enough time to play it."

Shane's eyes started to twinkle. "Now let me see if I've got this straight," he teased. "There's the Definitely Yes and the Probably Yes, and maybe we'll use all of them and maybe we won't, but we should probably stack them together." He choked back a laugh, then went on, "Then there's the Maybe Maybes and the Probably Nos. We could probably put them together with the Definitely Nos. Or do you think maybe we should definitely keep them separate?"

"*Maybe* we should . . ." Melanie began, but she was laughing too hard to go any further. She swayed toward Shane and felt his arm slip around her. They stood together, laughing softly for a moment. Then, as their laughter subsided, Shane tipped her chin upward and kissed her gently on the lips.

It was a wonderful kiss, Melanie thought. A perfect kiss. She felt tingly all over. As she opened her eyes, she was aware of soft sounds in the background and wondered briefly what she would say if her parents walked in at this very moment. Or if Jeffy came in and shrieked, "They're kissing! They're kissing!" Trying not to panic, she pulled her gaze away from Shane and looked quickly toward the door to the family room. Thankfully no one was there. She breathed a huge sigh of relief.

"I wonder if I could ask you a favor?" Shane said.

He asked the question casually, but his arm was still around her.

She smiled up at him again. "Sure."

"Well," he began, "since the records are all separated into categories, I thought maybe I should leave the Definitely Yeses and the Probably Yeses with you so that I won't have to worry about getting them mixed up again."

"But most of your favorite songs are Yeses," said Melanie. "What if you want to listen to them?"

"Couldn't I come over here and listen to them?"

Melanie blushed. "Of course," she said, hoping he realized how sincerely she meant it. "You can come over anytime you want to."

"Great," he said. "I was hoping that's what you'd say."

They finished the plate of brownies and talked for a little while longer before Shane called his dad to come after him. When he had gone, Melanie picked up the stack of records and carried them to her room for safe-keeping. Last night Scott had kissed her. Tonight Shane had. They were two of the cutest and most super boys in Wacko Junior High, and they both liked *her*. She hugged the records and whirled around the room, feeling like the luckiest girl alive.

CHAPTER

13

*A*t the football game the next afternoon, Melanie made sure she spent the time when the squad wasn't cheering with Dekeisha, Alexis, and Mandy. She also got in lots of flirt time with both Scott and Shane and shot big smiles at Garrett Boldt whenever he was close by photographing the action on the field.

She was doing it all for The Fabulous Five's benefit, of course. Well, mostly, anyway. She couldn't tell if Jana, Katie, and Christie had seen it all from their seats in the bleachers, but Beth, who was on the cheerleading squad, too, couldn't possibly have missed it. It had to be getting obvious to them that their cool treatment of her wasn't fazing her one little bit. Who knows? she thought wryly. Maybe *I'm* starting to be the one who doesn't have time for *them*.

To make matters even better, just before halftime Derek Travelstead called out hello to her from the stands, and she waved her pom-pons at him. She had been noticing him more and more lately, thinking how cute he was and trying to decide if he really did look like Kirk Cameron, after all.

After the game Melanie trudged back to the locker room alongside Mandy and Dekeisha. They were talking about the game, but she stayed quiet. She hadn't been able to shake the tiredness she had been feeling for several days. Some of the acrobatics in the cheers had seemed harder than usual, and now she was even considering skipping Bumpers. Just a teensy little nap would make her feel so much better. But still, if she didn't go to Bumpers after the game, she would not only miss a victory celebration, but also a perfect chance to show off her popularity to the rest of The Fabulous Five.

At Bumpers the jukebox was playing full blast when she picked up her Coke at the order counter and headed for the cheerleaders' table. A quick swallow of the frosty beverage felt good on her fiery throat. The sore throat she had awakened with yesterday had persisted, and yelling her lungs out at the football game hadn't helped it one bit.

She sat down between Alexis and Mandy just as Laura McCall was saying, "Did you see that terrific tackle Shane made in the second quarter? He's such a hunk. I certainly would have hated to be the guy he tackled. Well . . . sort of, anyway." She glanced around the table with a grin that said clearly that she wasn't talking about a football tackle this time.

Girls were laughing and mentioning other cute boys on the Wakeman team and commenting on what hunks they were, but Melanie sat fuming and gulping her Coke. How dare Laura talk about Shane like that, she thought. She acts as if he's her personal property.

"Does anybody have a date for the dance yet?" asked Tammy Lucero before Melanie could think of a good reply for Laura. Tammy was the world's biggest gossip, and she was always digging for information.

"I do," piped up Dekeisha. "Dan Bankston took me to the movie last night, and on the way home he asked me to go with him." She looked around proudly as a couple of cheerleaders hammed it up, swooning over the mention of Dan Bankston, who was the center on the Wakeman Warriors and known sometimes as The Hulk.

"Scott asked me after the publicity committee meeting Thursday night," bragged Melanie. "And when I said yes, he kissed me." She had put that last part in for Laura's benefit, and she could see by Laura's expression that her words had hit their mark.

"Big deal!" spat Laura. She tossed a superior look toward Melanie. "I think Shane is going to ask me. He certainly acts like it, and he's been hanging around a lot."

Melanie was so angry that she wouldn't have been surprised if smoke had billowed out of her ears and flames had shot out of her mouth when she opened it to speak.

"Well, he certainly wasn't hanging around you last night. He was at my house." She paused, gleefully watching Laura try to regain her composure. "We were picking out the music for the dance since we're both on the music committee. He didn't act as if he was interested in asking you or anyone else to the dance . . . especially when he kissed me good night."

In the moment of silence that followed this announcement, Melanie stood, picked up her Coke, and marched triumphantly out the door. She would have loved to stick around and see Laura's face when the words sunk in and hear how jealous everyone was of her popularity, but it was much more dramatic to make an exit now. It's the same sort of theatrical thing Beth would do, she mused. Of course Beth had been sitting at the table, too, and she would run and tell The Fabulous Five that Melanie was so popular that she had been kissed by two boys in one week. Things couldn't be working out better, she thought.

She went to bed early that evening, remembering fleetingly that this was the night she had asked her friends to sleep over. They had all turned her down, saying they were busy with other things. The memory still hurt, but so did her throat, and her head was throbbing again, too. In some ways she was almost relieved to be able to slip between the covers and drift off to sleep whenever she felt like it.

She tried to do her homework Sunday afternoon, but she kept dozing off every time she started to read. Late in the afternoon Shane called to check on an album that he thought he might accidentally have left at her house Friday night. When she told him it wasn't there, she thought about inviting him over for a while, but she was too tired to make conversation, even with Shane.

She managed to drag herself to school Monday morning. Her mother had tried to get her to stay home, saying that she looked like death warmed over, but there was going to be a quiz in English and it was the final day of dissecting in biology. There was no way she could afford to miss it.

That night she even made it to the refreshments committee meeting, again over her parents' protests. She was a little surprised when Christie motioned her to an empty chair on her left and chatted during the meeting as if everything were the same in The Fabulous Five. Christie even suggested that Melanie volunteer some of her mother's famous brownies for the dance.

Melanie was the last one to reach the pay phone after the meeting broke up at a little after ten o'clock. Randy was just hanging up.

"I'll give you a ride home," he offered.

"Great," she said. "I know my dad will appreciate not having to come out after me at this hour."

She wondered briefly if he would offer Christie a ride, too, but she was nowhere around. She must have already gone, Melanie thought. Steve Hernandez was also gone, and only Curtis and Melissa McConnell were standing by the door when she left with Randy.

When Melanie awoke the next morning, she could scarcely lift her head off the pillow. Her head no longer throbbed. It pounded. Her throat was on fire, and one look in the bathroom mirror showed that her glands were so swollen that her neck was twice its normal size.

"Oh, no," she moaned as she staggered back to her room and fell into bed. "I'm *sick*."

When her mother took her temperature a little while later, it was 103 degrees. "I'll call the doctor and see if I can get you in to see him right away," she said, patting Melanie reassuringly. Then she added, "I knew I shouldn't have let you go out so much lately."

"Did you call the attendance office to tell them I'll be absent?" Melanie asked, and then both of them laughed at the way her swollen throat made her voice sound more like a croak.

"Yes," said her mother. "Now you just rest, and everything will be okay."

Dr. Garroway checked her over carefully as he had done so many times since she was small. Finally he smiled sympathetically and said, "I think we'd better take a little blood out of your finger and run a couple of tests on it. I have a sneaking suspicion from the looks of things and from what your mother tells me about your schedule lately that you just may have come down with mononucleosis. It isn't fun," he said with a wink, "but it isn't fatal, either."

Melanie stared at the end of her finger and flinched as Dr. Garroway made a tiny prick and drew a few drops of blood up into a small glass tube. Mononucleosis? she thought, feeling instantly panicky. Wasn't that the same as mono? *The kissing disease?*

CHAPTER

14

*T*he phone was ringing when Melanie and her mother got home from the doctor's office. It was 4:15 in the afternoon, so Melanie knew the call was for her, but her mother shooed her away from the phone.

"You get on up to bed, young lady," she said with mock seriousness. "I'll answer it, and if it's for you, I'll tell them you'll call back after you've rested for a while."

For once in her life Melanie was too tired to care about the phone. She nodded gratefully and trudged up the stairs, barely hearing what her mother was saying.

"Hi, Alexis. Yes, she's here, but she can't come to the phone right now. We've just come from seeing Dr. Garroway, and he said she has mononucleosis. Yes, that's right. Mono. She has to rest now, but she'll call you back later."

Tumbling into bed, Melanie fell into a deep sleep. She slept through dinner, and sometime after dark her mother awakened her and offered her a bowl of soup.

"No, thanks," she said drowsily, and then turned over and slept through the night.

She was still groggy when she awoke the next morning, and her tongue felt dry and tasted as if an entire army of ants had marched across it. Dr. Garroway had given her some medication and told her to get plenty of rest and liquids. For once, his advice wouldn't be hard to follow.

She started to get out of bed when she remembered his diagnosis. Mononucleosis. The kissing disease. She sank back against her pillows. She had heard a lot about mono. Kids made jokes about it all the time, and everyone always said that kissing was the way you caught it.

"But I couldn't have gotten it from Scott or Shane," she insisted, saying the words half aloud. "I was already starting to feel sick before I kissed either one of them."

Melanie moped around her bedroom all day long, napping now and then, but mostly staring at the ceiling and thinking about the kissing disease.

"Where *did* I get it?" she asked herself over and over.

She thought about Scott and Shane again. Friday night had been the first time Shane had ever kissed her, but Scott had kissed her twice before. The last time had been when he took her home after Laura McCall's party, but that had been weeks ago. The first time had been before that, in sixth grade when they went to a movie together. Those two kisses had been too long ago to make her sick now, and the kiss after the publicity committee meeting had been too close.

Next she thought about her parents. She kissed them lots of times and they kissed her back. They gave each other kisses good-bye and sometimes kisses hello. But who ever heard of getting the kissing disease from your parents?

I dream about kissing cute boys, she mused. Boys like Garrett and Derek and, of course, Scott and Shane. In fact, sometimes I spend practically all day long having daydreams about dates and kissing. "No, silly," she scolded herself out loud. "You can't get real diseases from daydreams."

She racked her brain for another idea. What about the parent project and Scott's walrus? She considered that for a while. She and Scott had been mother and father to Scott's stuffed walrus as part of the Family Living class project. It was supposed to teach them responsibility, and either she or Scott had to be with the "baby" at all times. Melanie remembered how she had cuddled the walrus when it was her turn to take care of it. Could she have come into contact with some germs then? Of course not, she assured herself. Nothing of Scott's would have *germs* on it.

But germs . . . , she thought. There was another place she could have gotten germs: in the biology lab. She sat up in bed at the idea. Why hadn't she thought of it before? Wasn't Mr. Dracovitch always talking about the importance of washing their hands before and after working on the specimens? Maybe she had forgotten once and had gotten the kissing disease from touching Shane's and her cow's eyeball! The idea was so absurd that she burst out laughing.

It must be a mistake, she concluded. There was no way she could possibly have mono. Maybe she should ask Dr. Garroway to take another test, even if it meant getting her finger stuck a second time.

After school the phone rang again. A couple of minutes later her mother popped her head in the door and said, "It's for you, honey. Do you feel like talking to Beth?"

Melanie's heart leapt. One of her friends from The Fabulous Five was calling? Maybe Beth had heard that Melanie was sick, and she really did care, after all.

"Sure," she said. "I'll be right down."

"How are you feeling?" Beth asked eagerly when Melanie said hello.

"A little loopy right now," she answered, and chuckled. "I'm so weak that coming down the stairs just now was a real adventure. I should be okay in a few days, though."

"That's good," said Beth. Then, in a cautious voice, she asked, "Is what I heard at school today true?"

Melanie frowned. "What did you hear?"

"That you have mono."

There was silence on both ends of the line for a moment. Then Beth went on, "Alexis said she called your house yesterday, and your mom said you couldn't come to the phone because you had mononucleosis. Is it true?"

Melanie's thoughts were churning. She had heard her mother talking to Alexis, but she had been so tired that she had forgotten. How could my own mother do such a thing to me? she wondered. Now everybody will know.

Melanie sighed. "It's true," she admitted. "But I'll die if *everybody* finds out. Has Alexis told very many kids?"

Now it was Beth's turn to sigh. "Well, I don't know exactly whom she's told, but she was talking about it in the cafeteria today. You know what kind of scene that is. Almost anybody could have heard her. How did you catch mono, anyway?"

"I don't know," Melanie admitted with a catch in her voice. "I honestly don't know."

They talked for a few minutes longer, and just before they hung up, Beth told her that Sirloin Snake had finally been found. "The custodian spotted him behind the furnace," she said. "He was all curled up sleeping just like Mr. Dracovitch said he would be."

"Great," Melanie said halfheartedly. "Now every-body can put their feet on the floor again."

Even the good news about Mr. Dracovitch's snake didn't cheer Melanie up. All she could think about for the rest of the day was mononucleosis—the kissing dis-ease—and what everyone at school was probably say-ing about her. Especially Laura McCall. There was no way that Laura and the rest of The Fantastic Foursome would miss making the most out of her predicament.

The phone rang again just before bedtime. Melanie's stomach was churning as her mother called her to the phone. She dreaded talking with someone else from Wakeman about her illness.

It was Dekeisha. "Hi, Melanie," she began. "Are you feeling well enough to talk? Everyone is saying that you have mono."

For a second Melanie considered denying it, and saying instead that she only had a cold. If only her mother hadn't told Alexis the truth, she thought for the umpteenth time that day.

"I do have mono," she finally answered, adding quickly, "but the doctor said it's a *very* mild case. What's new at school?"

"That's partly why I called," Dekeisha said. "Laura McCall and her friends were saying all kinds of things about you today. Laura says that you've started an epi-demic at school."

"What!" shrieked Melanie.

"Well," continued Dekeisha cautiously, "at cheer-leading practice Laura told everyone that you were bragging at Bumpers on Saturday about kissing Scott and Shane. And Melissa McConnell said she saw you get a ride home with Randy Kirwan from the refreshments committee meeting Monday night. Chandra Sharp saw you flirting with Derek Travelstead at the decorations committee meeting and told Tammy Lucero all about it in biology class today. So The Fantastic Foursome says that there's no telling how many other boys you've infected with the kissing disease."

Melanie was speechless. Somehow she managed to thank Dekeisha for calling and got back to her room. There she stood in the middle of the floor, shaking with anger and humiliation. The nerve of Laura McCall, accusing her of infecting boys with mono, of starting an epidemic!

A new wave of tiredness swept over her, and she sank onto her bed again. She had been so busy trying to figure out how she had caught the kissing disease herself that she hadn't even thought about the possibility of passing it on to someone else. What if she *had* given it to Scott? What would he do?

"He'll hate me the rest of his life, that's what!" she muttered aloud.

And what about Shane? She closed her eyes and imagined his coming to her house to pick up his albums wearing a doctor's breathing mask and rubber gloves. "I must disinfect these before I play them again," he said as he carried them out in a cardboard box marked CONTAMINATED in big red letters.

Maybe they would have to disinfect the whole

school. She thought back to the time a few years ago when she had found an abandoned litter of kittens, put them into a box next to the dryer, and one had died of distemper. The vet had told them to make a mixture of bleach and water and disinfect the laundry room. Would Mr. Bell, the principal, hand out buckets of bleach water and sponges to every seventh-grader with instructions to disinfect Wacko Junior High just as if she were a stray kitten with distemper?

Tears rolled down her cheeks. She brushed them away, but more followed. What if Laura was right and the boys she had kissed really *did* get sick? All the other boys would run when she got near them. Nobody would want to sit beside her in class or stand near her in the cafeteria line. She'd be so embarrassed that she'd die. How could she possibly go back to school?

Melanie felt more alone and friendless than she ever had in her life. Where were her best friends in The Fabulous Five now that she needed them desperately? Busy! she thought angrily. Busy going their own separate ways.

CHAPTER

15

$\mathcal{F}$or the rest of the week Melanie stayed home from school resting and taking her medication. And worrying. Especially after she finally heard from the rest of The Fabulous Five. Jana was first. She called the day after Beth had.

"Hi, Mel. How are you feeling?" she began in a nervous voice.

"A lot better," Melanie assured her. She had made up her mind that no matter what people thought, she was going to act as if hardly anything were wrong.

"Great. I was really sorry to hear that you're sick," said Jana. "Beth said . . ." Jana hesitated, sounding more nervous than ever. "Beth said that you really do have mono."

Melanie frowned. "I think Dr. Garroway made a mistake on the test. I'm not nearly so tired, and my throat isn't quite as sore or swollen as it was."

"That's good. When do you think you'll be back to school?"

"I don't know yet," Melanie said with a sigh. "But I can't wait. This house is beginning to feel like a prison. Let's change the subject. What's going on at school? Do you know any juicy gossip?"

"Not really," said Jana. She hesitated again. "There is one thing I wanted to ask you though. . . ."

"Sure," said Melanie.

"Is it true that Randy gave you a ride home from the refreshments committee meeting Monday night?"

What! thought Melanie. Little explosions went off in her brain, sending red fireworks blazing before her eyes.

"Yes, he *did* give me a ride home. But for your information, we sat on opposite sides of the backseat, and I *did not* kiss him and give him mononucleosis!"

"Melanie! I didn't mean . . ."

Melanie didn't give Jana a chance to finish saying what she meant. It was pretty obvious. Jana *was* worried that Melanie had given Randy the kissing disease, no matter how hard she tried to hide it. Hanging up the receiver, Melanie trudged back to her room feeling worse than ever.

The phone rang again a little later. When her mother

called up to her, saying it was Katie, she braced to hear for the zillionth time that she was boy crazy. Katie was like an absolute broken record, always making a big thing out of the fact that Melanie was interested in a lot of boys. This business about mono has probably really set her off, thought Melanie. But Katie surprised her.

"I thought you ought to know that Laura McCall and the rest of The Fantastic Foursome are wagging their tongues all over school making sure that every-body knows you've started an epidemic of the kissing disease," she said. Melanie even thought she sounded a little sympathetic.

"I know how it feels to be gossiped about," Katie went on. "It happened to me when I first joined Teen Court. Remember?"

Melanie did remember. Lots of kids had said that Katie played favorites, getting her friends off with light punishments and really sticking it to kids she didn't like. That wasn't true, of course. Katie was the fairest person she knew.

"I remember," she said softly. "Thanks for telling me."

"Well . . . anyway . . ." Katie fumbled, and Mel-anie knew her friend didn't quite know what to say next. Finally she cleared her throat and added, "I also wondered if you need for me to drop off your assign-ments after school tomorrow?"

"Thanks," said Melanie. "But Mom stopped by the school today and got them." She started to add that Katie could come over anyway if she wanted to, then changed her mind. She wasn't ready to face anybody yet.

Christie was the only one of The Fabulous Five who hadn't called, Melanie mused before she went to sleep that night. But it didn't matter. What could Christie add to what the other three had said, that everybody in Wacko was talking about her and how she had the kissing disease.

The weekend was dreadfully long. In fact it was the longest one she could ever remember. She knew that everyone else was at the football game on the beautiful, fall Saturday afternoon, having fun without her while she had been sent to her room to take a nap. The cheerleaders would be cheering. The fans would be yelling. And then everybody would head for Bumpers after the game. Not only that, probably no one would miss her one little bit or think about her staying at home with her face and neck puffed out like a toad.

She tried to ignore the clock beside her bed. She didn't want to know when it was time for everybody to be at Bumpers. And she certainly didn't want to think about Laura flirting with Shane. Would Scott be looking around for someone different to ask to the dance? She didn't want to think about that either. But she couldn't help it, any more than she could help looking at the clock and picturing everything else that was going on at Bumpers. As the afternoon shadows grew long, she lay back against the pillows in her darkening bedroom and cried.

* * *

By Monday morning Melanie's temperature was back to 98.6 degrees for the second day in a row, and the swelling in her neck was gone.

"I think you can go back to school today if you're feeling well enough," her mother announced at breakfast.

First the good news, thought Melanie. I do feel well enough to go back. But now for the bad news. I'm scared to death of what everyone will say.

She gave her mother a noncommittal shrug and stared at her toast.

"What is that supposed to mean?" her mother asked gently. "Cold feet?"

Melanie kept her eyes downward. "Well, I feel okay now," she said, emphasizing the word *now*. "But what if I start feeling sick again in the middle of class?"

"Call me, and I'll come and get you," said Mrs. Edwards. "I really do think you should try, though, even if it's just for half a day."

"I don't know . . ." she said, but a little while later she climbed into the front seat of the car beside her mother and sat in silence as they drove to school.

When they reached Wakeman Junior High, Mrs. Edwards pulled up in front and stopped in the unloading zone. Melanie looked across the school ground. Kids she knew were milling around everywhere. She could see the rest of The Fabulous Five at their corner of the fence. Scott Daly was sliding his ten-speed into the bicycle rack. Alexis and Kim were sitting on the front step talking. It looked like any ordinary day.

A car honked impatiently behind them.

"You'd better get going, honey," her mother said softly.

Melanie nodded and opened the door. Just then she spotted The Fantastic Foursome standing near the gum tree. They were all looking in her direction. She stiffened, thinking that she would give almost anything to become instantly invisible, and climbed out of the car.

CHAPTER

16

*N*o one seemed to notice her at first. Melanie walked stiffly across the grounds in the opposite direction of the gum tree where Laura and her friends stood watching her, desperately hoping that everyone would just leave her alone. If she could get to the fence where The Fabulous Five were, everything would probably be okay. Surely they wouldn't desert her now. Even if the clique was starting to break up, hadn't they been friends practically forever?

Melanie kept on walking, concentrating on putting one foot in front of the other. Her legs felt as if they belonged to someone else and might go off in different

95

directions if she didn't force each one to keep moving straight ahead.

"HEY! LOOK WHO'S HERE!"

Melanie froze and jerked her head up to see who had spoken. Clarence Marshall was blocking her path. His hair was hanging in his eyes, and he was clutching his throat with both pudgy hands and pretending to gag.

"IT'S HER! IT'S HER! THE KISS OF DEATH!" he shrieked.

Everybody was watching, but nobody else said anything. Slowly groups of kids turned away from her, looking back over their shoulders at her and whispering among themselves. *The kiss of death*, she thought. That's what they all think.

After an eternity she heard someone else call her name.

"Hey, Melanie! Come over here." It was Katie, and she was motioning to Melanie to join them at the fence. Katie was the only one of The Fabulous Five smiling. The other three were exchanging nervous glances among themselves.

With a sigh, Melanie threw Clarence a drop-dead look and hurried toward them, but it didn't take her long to wish that she had gone to her locker instead. Katie asked her how she was feeling, and then the five of them lapsed into an uncomfortable silence, looking at the ground, at the school building, at the fence— anywhere but at each other. It was obvious to Melanie that her friends didn't know what to say to her. To make matters worse, she didn't know what to say to them, either. She didn't even know if they believed the terrible gossip that Laura McCall was spreading about her. Jana might, since she had called to ask about Melanie's riding home from the committee meeting with Randy. Maybe Christie did, too. After all, Jon was on the music committee with her. Finally the bell rang, and Melanie said a quick good-bye and headed toward the school.

The rest of the day was the pits. Every time she saw Laura or one of her friends, they would smirk and give her knowing looks or whisper to each other behind their hands. Most of the boys stared at her as if they were convinced she was the carrier of a dread disease and they would catch it if they even opened their mouths to say hello. Scott and Shane both spoke to her, but even they were hesitant and kept their distances, and Melanie noticed that Shane looked relieved when Mr. Dracovitch announced that they wouldn't be returning to the dissecting tables for a while.

Melanie was glad that Scott and Shane were both in school, which meant that they hadn't actually gotten her mono already, but she couldn't help secretly watching them every time she got the opportunity. She needed to see if either of them looked pale or acted as if they were coming down with something. But both of them seemed okay. So far, so good, she thought. She would have to keep her fingers crossed for tomorrow.

She didn't bother to go to the cafeteria at noon. No one would want her at their table. Instead, she got her lunch out of her locker and went out onto the school ground to eat by herself. The air was chilly as she looked around for a place to sit. A ninth-grade boy and girl were perched on the steps, gazing romantically at each other. The only tree nearby was the gum tree, and she certainly didn't want to sit under it.

Melanie stopped and looked at the gum tree. Even though most of its leaves had already fallen for the winter, it was almost pretty with its bark covered with bright gobs of pink and green and orange and blue and yellow chewing gum stuck there by students before going into class every morning. Still, everybody talked about how gross the tree was, and getting close enough to touch somebody clsc's gum was avoided at all cost.

"I know just how you feel," Melanie whispered to the tree, and then she looked around self-consciously to make sure no one was near enough to hear.

Scuffing out to the fence, she turned her back on the school and sat down on the cold ground. Using her biology book for a table, she pulled her sandwich out of the bag and took a bite. She glanced at the book and thought about Mr. Dracovitch. He was an outcast, too. Kids called him Dracula and made jokes behind his back. She had even done it herself. And now the dance committee was going to play an even bigger joke on him by asking him to chaperon the monster dance. Everyone would be talking behind his back, too. She sighed. Poor Mr. Dracovitch. I almost wish that there weren't going to be a dance, for both our sakes.

Melanie was leaning against the fence, still thinking about her and Mr. Dracovitch's predicaments, when

Beth came up to her. Her heart skipped a beat as Beth dropped to one knee beside her and asked, "What are you doing out here instead of eating in the cafeteria with the rest of us?"

"I didn't think anyone would want to sit with me after the silent treatment I got at the fence this morning," said Melanie, looking away.

Beth hesitated before she spoke. "I guess nobody knew exactly what to say to . . ." She lowered her eyes.

"To someone with the kissing disease and who goes around kissing boys and starting epidemics? Is that what you mean?" Melanie asked angrily.

"It's Laura and the rest of The Fantastic Foursome who are talking about epidemics," Beth argued. "They're really making a big deal out of it and scaring kids—especially boys—into thinking they're going to get sick if they even hang around you." Her voice softened. "Christie and Katie and Jana and I don't really believe them, and we tell everybody that we don't. It's just that we don't know very much about mononucleosis, either. We don't know what else to say."

"That's okay," Melanie said halfheartedly. She couldn't really blame them, she supposed. She gathered her books and stood up, and as she turned to head toward the school, she looked back and gave Beth a weak smile. "Thanks, anyway."

Things didn't get much better during the afternoon, although Dekeisha and Mandy both said hello in the halls. By the time Melanie got home from school she was exhausted. She had barely gotten through her classes with everyone staring at her and acting as if she were poison. She finished her homework thinking that all she wanted to do was go to sleep and forget all about Wacko Junior High and about The Fabulous Five and mono and dances. She couldn't go to the dance committee meetings anymore because Dr. Garroway had prescribed a lot of rest. She was almost ready to climb into bed when her mother called her to the phone.

"It's Christie," said Mrs. Edwards. "She sounds really anxious to talk to you."

Melanie frowned and leaned against the wall. Christie had hardly spoken to her at school today. Why on earth was she calling now? She considered telling her mother that she didn't feel like talking to anyone. But instead she put the receiver to her ear and said in a tired voice, "Hi, Christie. What do you want?"

"I've got something important to tell you." Christie's voice sounded excited. "Really important. Can you talk?"

"What's it about? I'm really beat."

"You're going to want to hear this," Christie assured her. And then she added mysteriously, "It's about the kissing disease."

CHAPTER

17

*M*elanie's scalp tingled as if a thousand daddy longlegs spiders were dancing in her hair. "What *about* the kissing disease?" she whispered.

"Well," Christie began importantly, "my brother Mike called a little while ago to say that he's coming home this weekend. He's in medical school, you know."

"I know! I know!" insisted Melanie, slapping the wall behind her impatiently. "What about the kissing disease?"

"I'm getting to that. Anyway, I answered the phone, and after he told me he would be home for the weekend, I asked him if he had studied anything about mononucleosis in medical school yet. At first he thought I had it, and he laughed, calling it the kissing disease and asking me where I got it."

Christie paused, and Melanie's heart sank. This didn't sound like anything she wanted to hear. She was about to say so when Christie started talking again.

"So I said, no, I don't have it, but do you really get it from kissing? And he laughed again and said, no, that's just a myth. It's really a virus that makes kids sick when they get too tired and run-down and don't eat right or take care of themselves. He said it's really hard to catch from someone else, and that the odds are about a billion to one against getting it from kissing. Isn't that terrific!"

Melanie was too weak-kneed to answer right away, and she slid slowly down the wall and sank to the floor as a giddy smile spread across her face. If you couldn't get it from kissing, then she hadn't passed it on to Scott or Shane, either.

"Are you there?" demanded Christie. "Answer me!"

"I'm here," said Melanie.

"You didn't faint, did you?" Christie asked anxiously. "Maybe you'd better get back to bed."

"I didn't faint. In fact I've never felt so great in my life. And what's more, no matter what that witch Laura McCall and her friends are trying to spread, I *couldn't* have started an epidemic of the kissing disease!"

"Right," said Christie. "The trouble is that she has

practically everybody convinced that you did and that you're a walking disaster."

Melanie's happy mood fizzled away like a balloon with a slow leak. "Is it that bad?"

"Worse," said Christie. "Don't tell anyone I told you this, but at noon I overheard Elizabeth Harvey telling some girls that she had accidentally touched your locker with her left hand and that she was heading straight to the girls' room to wash it off."

"What!" shrieked Melanie. "I thought mono was supposed to be a *kissing* disease, not a *touching* disease."

"That was before Laura and her gossipy friends started talking about it," conceded Christie.

Neither of them said anything for a moment. Then Melanie asked in a small voice, "What am I going to do?"

"I don't know yet, but I'm thinking," Christie assured her. "And so are the rest of The Fabulous Five. I've already talked to them. Meet us at the fence in the morning. Maybe by then one of us will have thought of a way to stop the lies that Laura and her friends are telling."

Melanie tumbled into bed as soon as they hung up, but she had too much on her mind to go to sleep. She wanted to hug herself with joy now because Christie had found out that mono wasn't really a kissing disease, and because Christie and the others wanted to help fight the rumors Laura had started. But at the same time, she felt confused. The real reason she had

gotten mono was because she had been going to all
those dance committee meetings so she could make
new friends and had been going out with cute boys
and trying to be popular. And the reason she had
worked herself silly trying to be popular was because
she had thought that her old friends in The Fabulous
Five didn't want to be friends with her anymore, and
she wanted to show them that she didn't need them
either.

No, she corrected herself. I didn't just work myself
silly. I worked myself into a big, fat case of mononucleosis. And for what? Just so that The Fabulous
Five can help me get out of all the trouble that I created
for myself! The thought was so funny that she rolled
over onto her back and giggled in the dark.

When Melanie got to the fence the next morning, the
rest of The Fabulous Five were already there. For the
first time in weeks they acted genuinely glad to see her,
gathering around her and asking how she felt.

"Lots better," she said, "but I still don't know what
to do about Laura's lies. Does anyone have any ideas?"

"No," confessed Christie. "I thought and thought
and thought last night, but I couldn't come up with
anything."

"Me, either," said Beth.

"I guess all we can do is talk to as many kids as possible and tell them that mono isn't really a kissing disease," said Melanie.

"But who's going to believe us?" argued Katie. "They all know Melanie is one of our best friends. They'll think we're just saying it to make her look better. What we need is someone with authority to tell them."

Everyone sighed and lapsed into silence again. Melanie knew that Katie was right. There was no use in going around saying one thing when Laura and her friends would be saying the opposite. Just as many kids would believe Laura as would believe them. What good would that do? What they needed was someone with authority. But who?

"What about the school nurse?" asked Jana.

"She visits a different school every day," Melanie reminded her. "This is only Tuesday, and she won't get to Wacko until Friday. I can't wait that long."

Jana shrugged apologetically and everyone went back to thinking again.

"I know this is far out," Katie said, "but what about Mr. Dracovitch?"

"Get real," Beth said incredulously.

"The biology teacher?" murmured Melanie.

"Sure," said Katie.

"Maybe you've got something," said Melanie. "He knows about all kinds of medical things. You should have heard what he told our class about eyeballs. And everybody believed him. I'll bet if he made a scientific announcement about mono's not being a kissing disease, kids would believe him about that, too."

"I don't know," said Jana, shaking her head.

"Wait a minute," said Katie. "It's a great idea. Let's at least go ask him. If we hurry, we can talk to him before the bell rings."

Melanie was still feeling weak from her illness so she trailed the others as they raced into the school and up the stairs to the biology lab. She kept her fingers crossed the whole way that he would be in his room by now, and her heart was pounding from both exertion and excitement when she peeked inside the laboratory door and saw him sitting at his desk.

"Mr. Dracovitch?" she asked softly.

He looked up and smiled at her. "Hi, Melanie. Come on in. Oh, I see you have friends with you. They're welcome, too."

"Go on," whispered Katie, nudging her forward. "We'll back you up."

Melanie took a deep breath and approached her teacher's desk while the others lingered near the door. He was looking at her kindly, but she couldn't help noticing for the zillionth time how his shiny, black toupee made him look exactly like Dracula. Why would anybody in her right mind go to him for help in putting a stop to untrue rumors? she wondered.

She shifted from one foot to the other, trying to find a way to begin. It all sounded so crazy when she tried to say it out loud.

"What can I do for you?" urged Mr. Dracovitch.

"Someone in this school is spreading terrible lies about why I've been sick, and I need scientific proof that mononucleosis *isn't* a kissing disease and that I *haven't* started an epidemic." Melanie blurted the words out, but once she did, she began to feel better. She told him the whole story, leaving out only the names of the guilty so that he wouldn't think that her motive was only revenge.

Mr. Dracovitch listened quietly. When she had finished talking, he leaned back in his chair, touched the tips of his fingers together, and looked at her thoughtfully.

"Hmmm," he said at last. "I can see that you do have a problem and a serious one at that. It isn't much fun to have vicious rumors spread about you."

He paused, and Melanie swallowed hard and waited for him to go on. "I think I can help you," he said. Smiling, he motioned for her to come closer. Cupping his hands around his mouth, he whispered conspiratorially, "In case I can't find mononucleosis in any of my science books, is it okay if I check with your doctor?"

"Sure," she whispered back. "He's Dr. Garroway."

Melanie could hardly contain her happiness after she left Mr. Dracovitch's room. She didn't even mind that some kids stepped out of her way in the halls and others turned away and began whispering. She wasn't sure exactly how good old Dracula was going to help her, but she knew he would.

Homeroom period dragged on forever. Mrs. Clark, Melanie's homeroom teacher, took attendance, collected lunch money, and read the morning announcements just as she did every morning. "All right, students, please work on your homework assignments or sit quietly for the rest of the period," she said.

Just then the door opened and Miss Simone, the school secretary, came bustling into the room carrying a stack of papers. She took one off the top and thrust it toward Mrs. Clark.

"This is an additional announcement," said Miss Simone. "Please read it right away."

Mrs. Clark glanced at the announcement, looked surprised for an instant, and then said, "This is from Mr. Dracovitch."

Melanie sprang to attention like a jack-in-the-box as Mrs. Clark went on.

"'It has come to my attention that some incorrect information is circulating around Wakeman Junior High about mononucleosis. As your science teacher, I want to inform you that there is no scientific basis for believing that mono is a kissing disease.'"

Giggles and whispers interrupted Mrs. Clark, and Melanie could feel eyes turning to her.

"'Furthermore,'" Mrs. Clark went on reading. "'I have consulted with a prominent local physician, and he has confirmed that mononucleosis is a virus that attacks only the most hardworking, busy, and popular students.'"

Pandemonium broke loose as kids stamped and whistled and applauded. Everyone in the room was in an uproar except Melanie. She just leaned back against her seat and smiled.

CHAPTER

18

"You know, what Mr. Dracovitch said about mono's being a virus that attacks hardworking, busy, and popular kids is true," said Katie when The Fabulous Five met at Bumpers after school.

Melanie was only half listening. She was thinking about how much better her life had become since homeroom this morning. Laura McCall had gone around looking mad enough to spit hornets. Dekeisha and Chandra had both asked Melanie if she was feeling well enough to come back to the dance committee meetings. Scott had stopped at her table in the cafeteria to ask her if it was okay to double with Mark

Peters and Alexis Duvall for the dance, and Shane had slipped her a note in biology class saying that if she wasn't busy Friday night, he'd like to come over and listen to Definitely Yes and Probably Yes records with her. And then, after school the rest of The Fabulous Five had waited for her beside her locker so that they could all come to Bumpers together.

"I agree," Beth was saying to Katie. "Especially about the popular part. Mel, every time I looked at you, you were surrounded by kids. I didn't know that you had so many friends."

Melanie shrugged and took a long drink of her soda. Here it comes, she thought. I might as well level with them.

"You were the friends that were most important to me, but you were all changing and acting as if you didn't want to be around me anymore. I felt invisible. And no matter what subject I brought up, the rest of you seemed to want to talk about something else. Finally, I decided that you didn't want to be friends anymore, and that maybe The Fabulous Five was starting to break up. You were all too busy to care about me anymore, and that's why I started going around with a lot of other kids."

"To make us jealous?" asked Beth.

Melanie nodded and choked back tears. She wanted to say more, to talk about how lonely she had been, how left out she had felt, but she knew she would never be able to get the words out around the lump in her throat.

"I know exactly how you felt," said Jana. Melanie looked at her in surprise as she went on. "I felt all alone just before Mom and Pink got married. I wanted to talk to someone about how different things were going to be when I had to start sharing Mom with Pink all the time, but you guys just wanted to talk about the wedding."

Melanie listened in amazement as each one of her friends mentioned times when she had felt left out, too.

"You guys always seem to resent the time I spend with Jon," admitted Christie. "And I'll never forget how you guys nominated me for class president without even asking me how I felt about it."

"Not one of you ever wants to hear about Teen Court and how important it can be to Wakeman Junior High," said Katie.

Even Beth shrugged and said, "I can't see anything wrong with trying to help the Indians, but sometimes you guys act as if I've lost my mind." She sighed and added, "Sometimes it just seems better to do my own thing and go my own separate way."

Melanie rattled the ice in the bottom of her glass and stared at it. She was thinking about all the stories she had heard about friendships changing in junior high. *Changing*, she thought. That was the clue. Friendships changed, but they didn't have to end.

"I guess we don't always have to like exactly the same things to still be best friends," she said softly.

"Or spend every single waking moment together," offered Jana.

"You're right," said Christie. "As we get older, it's only natural that we'll start having separate interests."

"Absolutely," said Katie. "We're *friends*, not *clones!* The important thing is that we'll always care about each other and be there when one of us needs help."

Melanie nodded. "Just the way you came to my rescue. The important thing is that we've got to listen to each other from now on." She started feeling choked up again, but this time it was because she was happy. Raising her glass in triumph, she said, "We'll *always* be The Fabulous Five!"

Wacko Wonderland was a huge success, even though Melanie had a terrible time deciding what kind of costume to wear. She had thought about going as Elvira after she'd seen a costume at a discount store. Even there, the price was too high for her allowance, and so she racked her brain to come up with something clever that she could put together herself. Finally, she thought of the perfect idea.

The day of the dance she put on her chocolate-brown jogging suit. Then she glued little balls of yellow, green, blue, orange, and pink tissue paper all over it. Next, she found an old baseball cap that belonged to her dad. She cut a few short, bare branches off the maple tree in the back yard, glued on green construction-paper leaves, and attached the branches to the cap before setting it on her head.

"You're the gum tree!" shouted Scott when she opened the door for him a little while later.

"And you're a robot," she guessed. He was standing on the front step wrapped in aluminum foil from head to toe.

"Naw," he said. "I'm a mummy from outer space. But you were close."

There were all sorts of far-out monsters at the dance, milling around under ghostly pastel-colored streamers. Dozens of weird-looking space creatures hovered around the refreshment table. "Earth food! Earth food!" shouted one of them in a voice that sounded like Curtis Trowbridge's.

Taffy Sinclair was covered with puffy pink netting. "I'm a pink cloud," she said proudly.

Shane's costume was one of the biggest surprises of all.

"Look!" someone shouted. "Here comes a cow's eyeball!"

Shane stepped into the center of the room grinning broadly and wearing a huge, round papier-mâché ball that reached from his shoulders down to his knees. The front looked exactly like an eye with a pupil and iris inside a large white area that was surrounded by a fringe of black pipe-cleaner lashes. The rest of the ball was bluish-black just as the real eyeball had been. Kids were laughing and crowding around him.

"That's a terrific costume," said Melanie. "But

where's Igor? I thought he was going to help you with the music."

Shane gave her a helpless shrug. "It's his own fault. He was supposed to dress as my teardrop, but he said he'd look silly and refused to get into his costume."

Mr. Bell and Miss Dickinson moved around the crowd talking to first one monster and then another, but even though Melanie had been watching for him all evening, she couldn't spot the other chaperon, Mr. Dracovitch.

She still felt guilty. He had been so nice to help her get rid of the rumors that had been making her life so miserable, and yet kids were still calling him Dracula and saying he was a vampire behind his back. Asking him to be a chaperon at a monster dance seemed to her to make the insult worse.

Suddenly there was a commotion near the door. As she and Scott pushed forward, she could see a puff of smoke and hear kids gasp around the room. An instant later the smoke cleared and there he stood—*Dracula!* Melanie's heart stopped. He looked so *real*. His shiny, black toupee was pulled even lower than usual on his forehead, and his huge eyes were outlined in black. He was wearing a black cape lined in blood red, which he swirled about himself as he entered the room.

"What's going on?" whispered Scott, taking Melanie's hand.

"I don't know," she said, "but it's scary."

The next instant Dracula stopped stone still and held up his hand for silence. Then his face took on a

sinister grin, revealing long, sharp fangs. "I have heard
. . . that you students . . . know my secret," he began
in a raspy voice. "And so . . . I have come . . ." He
paused, raising his eyebrows and looking around the
room as a second wave of gasps filled the air.

To bite your neck. Melanie finished his sentence in her
mind as she held Scott's hand and squeezed it tight.

". . . TO CHAPERON YOUR DANCE! SO
HAVE FUN!" He threw back his head and laughed
again, but this time he didn't sound the least bit like a
monster. Melanie's mouth dropped open. She couldn't
believe it. He had known all along. And tonight he had
fooled them, playing a gigantic trick on everyone
there, and best of all, they were all laughing with him
because they loved it.

A little while later when the music was going and
everybody was dancing and having fun, Melanie saw
Mr. Dracovitch standing alone. She took a deep breath
and headed toward him. There was something she
needed to ask.

"Excuse me," she said timidly. "But why did you
help me out with the terrible things kids were saying
about me when you knew all along what they were
saying about you?"

"Do you mean that I'm a vampire?" he asked, and
raised one eyebrow.

Melanie nodded. It sounded even worse when Mr.
Dracovitch said it himself.

"Well, you see, Melanie, there are two different

kinds of rumors. The ones someone starts about you, and the ones you start about yourself."

Melanie looked at him with shocked disbelief, but before she could say anything, he went on, "That's right. I wanted kids to call me Dracula all along. I think it's terrific. It gets a lot more Wakeman kids interested in taking science classes. In fact," he said, slipping back into his Dracula voice, "they hang . . . on every word . . . that I say."

It was the biggest joke yet, and when Melanie thought about it the next day, she had to admit that Mr. Dracovitch was pretty cool. He had masqueraded as a vampire to get kids interested in science. He had let them talk about him and laugh about him without batting an eye.

"Now that's what I call being secure," she admitted out loud.

I'm a lot more secure now, too, she thought. When I was doubting The Fabulous Five's friendship, I was really doubting myself. It took the kissing disease to make me see the truth.

The kissing disease, she mused, and then smiled. She had learned the truth about that, too, and nothing could be more super—especially since she had danced with gorgeous Derek Travelstead last night and then given him her telephone number.

CHAPTER

19

*W*hen Miss Dickinson announced the homework assignment, Katie Shannon thought that she must have heard her teacher wrong. This was English Literature, she had thought, not Pop Culture 101.

"Making your own bumper stickers will help you to understand satire and how it is used in literature," Miss Dickinson had said, handing out long strips of paper. "Satire is simply sarcasm, usually cleverly written, that criticizes some aspect of the world. And of course, condensing it to fit your paper will help you say what you mean in a very few words."

Katie felt relieved when Miss Dickinson explained it

that way. Actually, she could think of lots of things in the world that needed criticizing, and doing it with bumper stickers just might turn out to be a lot of fun.

Joel Murphy's hand rocketed into the air, and the rest of his body looked as if it were going to follow. "I've got one already," he cried.

Miss Dickinson shook her head. "Write it down, Joel. You'll get plenty of opportunities to read your bumper sticker wisdom to the class tomorrow."

A lot of kids snickered, and Katie rolled her eyes to the ceiling. *I can just imagine what kind of macho slogan he came up with,* she thought.

The bell rang before Joel could protest, and the class filed into the hall.

"Some assignment, huh?" said Shawnie Pendergast, coming up beside Katie.

Katie smiled and glanced at Shawnie, glad to see that her eyes weren't red. Almost every morning Shawnie came to school looking as if she had been crying. Katie wasn't sure why, except that she had heard rumors that Shawnie's parents were unbelievably strict and that Shawnie had even threatened to leave home.

"I think it's going to be fun," said Katie. "It's our chance to make a statement about something we really believe in."

Shawnie's face brightened. "You've got a point," she said. "There are a few things I'm *dying* to say out loud. Maybe this is my chance."

Katie stopped at her locker and watched Shawnie

scuff on down the hall. She acts like a volcano that's about to blow, Katie thought, frowning.

Katie spent the entire evening working on her bumper sticker, and her wastebasket overflowed with ideas she had written down on pieces of scrap paper and then discarded. Finding the subject was the hardest part. There were so many things she cared about. The women's movement. Justice. Peace. Finally she settled on an idea, wrote it on her bumper sticker, and went to bed.

In English class the next day, everyone wanted to be first. Joel Murphy was his usual obnoxious self, waving his bumper sticker in the air and making grunting noises that sounded like a monkey to Katie.

"All right, Mona Vaughn, you may go first," said Miss Dickinson, ignoring Joel's antics.

Mona stood and unfurled her bumper sticker for the class to see. "It says, 'Help the hungry—keep them out of the school cafeteria!'"

The class thundered its applause and Miss Dickinson had to shout for everyone to be quiet.

"Marcie Bee, you're next."

Marcie looked nervous. "'Peace in the world or the world in pieces,'" she mumbled, holding her sticker down by her side.

"Hey! I've heard that before," shouted Steve Hernandez.

"This is supposed to be original," said Matt Zeboski.

"It's all I could think of," Marcie protested.

Katie raised her hand, and Miss Dickinson nodded. "'Nuclear war: the choice of the *last* generation!'" she said proudly. No one laughed at that one, and Katie sat down, satisfied that she had made the others think about something serious for a change.

"'School is a ball . . . *and a chain!*'" said Derek Travelstead, and the class was laughing again.

Finally Joel got his chance. "'A spare rib is another name for a useless woman.'"

The boys laughed at that one, and the girls booed. Katie seethed with anger.

Finally it was Shawnie's turn to read her sticker. She stood by her seat, and Katie noticed that her face was blotched, as if she had been crying again. Raising her sticker over her head, Shawnie spat out the words: "'*Empty the nation's prisons. Let your kid out of the house once in a while!*'"

Katie watched sadly as Shawnie crumpled back into her seat. What was the matter with the Pendergasts, anyway? she wondered. Did they really keep her a prisoner? No matter what, nobody should make their child that miserable.

Will Katie be able to help Shawnie deal with her situation at home? Or will Katie's sense of justice and fair play get her into more trouble than she can handle? Find out in *The Fabulous Five #8: THE RUNAWAY CRISIS.*

ABOUT THE AUTHOR

Betsy Haynes, the daughter of a former newswoman, began scribbling poetry and short stories as soon as she learned to write. A serious writing career, however, had to wait until after her marriage and the arrival of her two children. But that early practice must have paid off, for within three months Mrs. Haynes had sold her first story. In addition to a number of magazine short stories and the Taffy Sinclair series, Mrs. Haynes is also the author of *The Great Mom Swap* and its sequel, *The Great Boyfriend Trap*. She lives in Colleyville, Texas, with her children and husband, who is also an author.

Great FREE offer
just for you!

Join SNEAK PEEKS™!

Do you want to know what's new before anyone else? Do you like to read great books about girls just like you? If you do, then you won't want to miss SNEAK PEEKS™! Be the first of your friends to know what's hot ... When you join SNEAK PEEKS™, we'll send you FREE inside information in the mail about the latest books ... *before they're published!* Plus updates on your favorite series, authors, and exciting new stories filled with friendship and fun ... adventure and mystery ... girlfriends and boyfriends.

It's easy to be a member of SNEAK PEEKS™. Just fill out the coupon below ... and get ready for fun! It's FREE! Don't delay—sign up today!